I Want Golden Eyes

EMERGING VOICES FROM THE MIDDLE EAST

Series editor: *Dena Afrasiabi*

Other titles in this series include:

Thunderbird
I Saw Her in My Dreams
A Bed for the King's Daughter

I Want Golden Eyes

MARIA DAADOUCH

translated by
M Lynx Qualey & Sawad Hussain

This English translation copyright © 2025 by Marcia Lynx Qualey and Sawad Hussain

All rights reserved.
Printed in the United States of America.

Cover art & design by Noha Eilouti
Book design by Allen Griffith of Eye 4 Design

Library of Congress Control Number: 2024951085
ISBN: 9781477323359

Originally published as *'Uriid 'uyunan dhahabiya* in 2021

I Want Golden Eyes

1

Claws scratched at me. Fangs dug into my shoulder. And three or four winged arms dragged me out of my mother's embrace. All around me, wings flapped, while drool dripped onto my face. The smell made my stomach turn. My shirt was torn, and my book—which I had hidden in the folds of my clothes—fell to the ground. After that, everything was blood and ashes. I was ash. With everything left in my lungs, I yelled "Noooo!"

My eyes flew open. Had I really shouted that NO out loud? Or had it only been a cry inside my dream? My breaths came faster, and a cold sweat broke out behind my ears. The book was still in my hands: *Numbers and Dimensions*, by Dr. Zihni al-Ketbi.

The metacrystal disc on my wrist pulsed out the time: 6:03 a.m. Baba and Dima were already up. My sister glanced over and frowned. "Diyala, we can't be late. Get up. You know the checkpoint always takes at least an hour."

Like every morning, my sister Dima was standing in front of the mirror, tweezers in hand, grabbing hold of the stubborn hairs that popped out where she'd penciled in her violet eyebrows. After that, she spread a kiwi-colored powder over her cheeks. Apparently, kiwi was *the thing* this month. Baba injected his medicine into a vein and then dipped a silicone cup into the bucket we'd hung from the wall; it collected water that seeped out from the rock.

Our apartment was carved into the stone, and our government insisted that this stone-filtered water was safe to drink. And, well, usually, you shouldn't believe a single word our government says.

Then everyone was ready to go. Everyone except me. I tucked the book into the waistband of my pants and knotted the strings tight around my belly, feeling the book press against my stomach. I made an extra knot in the elastic to pull the book even closer, hoping it wouldn't fall out at the wrong moment. If that happened, it would be lights out for me. Here in the Burrow, no one was allowed to read books, except for the ones assigned in school. The penalty for breaking that law was death. But for me it felt like, if I didn't read, I might as well be dead.

I jumped down off the platform that served as my bed, hitting the ground. My platform was attached to the wall, and the only thing on it was my mattress. We didn't need blankets underground, since the temperature never dropped below eighty-five, no matter how cold it was up above. Baba and Dima's platforms were fixed to the walls next to mine.

Just then, the display ball hanging down from the ceiling beamed out an advertisement for a tinfoil dress. The

CHAPTER 1

commercial was on mute because, yesterday at bedtime, we'd set it to silent.

The bathroom, the display ball, the sleeping platforms, and Dima's dressing table and mirror were everything we had in Apartment #879. *Our* apartment. The 8 meant we were eight floors underground, and the 79 told you our place on that floor. I pulled a long, wide blouse out from one of the nooks that held our meager clothes, and I slipped it over my head without even tugging down on the zipper. Glancing down at my waist, I made sure the book didn't show under my shirt. Once I reached the front door with Dima and Baba, we all stepped out into Alley #8, joining the hundreds of other people who were headed off to work.

Alley #8 was the ring road that connected all 500 apartments on our floor. Above our floor, there were seven other floors, and below us, 52. All together, these sixty floors made up what we called the Burrow, where all of us Limiteds were crammed in together.

Like I said, our alley was a circle, and at its center was The Hollow. This, naturally, was the hole at the center of the Burrow. The only things in it were giant steel rods made of powerful nanoparticles. An elevator slid up and down these rods as it carried us Limiteds up to the surface of the earth. Up there was Quartzia, a city of quartz-built domes.

Today, we headed to Public Square 8, where the checkpoint was waiting for us. The only way to get to Quartzia was to take the elevator. And to ride in an elevator, you had to go through a screening. The problem with the screening was the guards: Griffin bats.

"Hurry *up*, before this line jams up the whole square," Dima said, dragging me by the arm. I grabbed Baba with my other arm, urging him to hurry, even though I felt sure that his shuffling steps couldn't go any faster. More and more Limiteds were pouring out of their apartments, and the crowd was growing bigger with every passing second. Each morning, we Limiteds headed for the elevators, and almost all of us headed out at the same time.

The Limiteds were the unfortunate ones whose brains, on the day of their birth, had scored less than 1111. The happy souls whose brains scored above this number got golden eyes from the National Iris Center. Golden-eyed people lived up above, in Quartzia. Sometimes, a child of high intelligence was born into a family of Limiteds, but it didn't happen to us. Baba, Dima, Mama (may she rest in peace), and I were all Limiteds. No golden eyes in our family. I wondered: How was this intelligence distributed? Was it in the genes? In the food? In your health? No one even asked anymore. Today, most people just worried about paying their monthly bills and staying out of the bats' claws.

We arrived at the bridge that connected our apartment's alley to the atrium around the elevator. Sunlight reached down from the glass dome above us, into the pit below, and the glow from above made the hovering Griffin-bat guards look like shadowy ghosts. I leaned on the bridge's railing

CHAPTER 1

and looked down toward the bottom of the pit—it was so deep that I couldn't see the end of it, only darkness. Something awful had happened down there, far below. It was something I didn't fully remember, but I still felt a chill every time I crossed the bridge. I couldn't manage to remember what had happened down there, no matter how hard I tried. Not even hypnosis could help me drag it out of the depths of my forgetting.

At the end of the bridge, we found the space around the elevator only half-full. If we had gotten there just ten minutes later, it would've been packed with hundreds of people. Quickly, we slipped into the line around the elevators. As soon as we were there, I breathed a sigh of relief. I pulled out a milk-flavored energy bar, the kind with calcium citrate, and handed it to Baba. I didn't like that he'd injected his medicine on an empty stomach, and now was the time to fix it. Baba took the bar from my hand and tapped my chin with the back of his pointer finger. Ever since his illness, when he lost the ability to speak, Baba had said thanks with his pointer finger. The doctor here in the Burrow said that Baba had what they called "Aggregate Multiple Sclerosis," which was an old disease with a new twist. I missed his old voice, and his old personality—from before he'd gotten sick! Now, I leaned down to kiss his pointer finger and gave him a small smile.

Dima had gotten sucked into watching the same commercial that had been playing over our heads every morning for the last two years. In it, there were two characters who looked like an attractive King and Queen of the Comoros. They embraced in front of the Floor 8 residents as a voice-over said, "Do you want to live a life of luxury? Have a modern home on the sweetest island on the planet? If you do, then all you have to do is put your name in for the Dreamland lottery!"

The announcement echoed against the Burrow's stone walls, creating a deafening roar. *If the Griffin bats don't kill us*, I thought, *then these ooey-gooey stupid government ads will.* On top of that, the announcements drowned out everything else, so that you couldn't hear what anyone was saying. Although, in truth, who even wanted to talk in the atrium, when Griffin bats were everywhere? The Griffin bats hung from the dark corners of the hollow, just waiting for us to make a mistake, so that they could pounce.

"Damn that Professor Griffin. I wish he'd never discovered Griffin bats a hundred years ago," I said, turning to Dima. "If he'd never existed, then these guards wouldn't have been made."

Instinctively, Dima jerked around, afraid that one of the Griffin guards might have heard us. People said that bats could hear the sound of the bite of energy bar sliding down Baba's throat, moving toward his stomach—but I thought they must be exaggerating. When they first "discovered" the Griffin bat back in 2008, people called it the Ugliest Creature on Earth. And, ever since then, the beasts had been earning that title.

CHAPTER 1

The Griffin guards were all clones of a single original. Scientists had given them a human brain, but also winged arms that ended in claws. Many of them carried a whip and would use it when necessary. Or when not necessary, too. Their faces were covered in nasty folds of raw skin. I guessed that they might have a nose, a mouth, eyes, or ears in there, but I could never make out any of their features. Their brains shot out sonar waves, and they struck everything around them. These waves bounced back and were caught by their wrinkled folds. From that, the Griffin bats could draw a mental map of the area. That was how they studied the movements of their victims.

Us.

Now, it was our turn to be scanned, and I felt my guts twist. I had smuggled hundreds of books past the guards, but I still couldn't get over the fear I felt every time I went through the checkpoint. They ran the device over Baba's forehead, then Dima's, and then it was my turn. I stood inside the purple circle, and the laser ray passed over my forehead. On the day we were born, the government had implanted a chip in our foreheads that carried all our information: our names, the names of our parents, and of course our intelligence score.

After a moment, the red curtain of light that had been blocking my path was lifted, and the way to the elevators was clear. I resisted the urge to touch the book tucked in the waistband of my pants as I passed the last Griffin guard near the elevator. I told myself, *The pages of the book won't move, so the sonar won't see it*, as I told myself to ignore the icy fear that had crept into my fingertips.

I tried to muster a confidence I didn't really feel, taking sure steps as I moved past the bat, until I reached the closed elevator door where Baba and Dima were waiting for me, crowded in with hundreds of other Limiteds. The bat was definitely monitoring my heartrate, but I was sure that everyone who passed by that thing felt their heart speed up with fear. Today, like other days, the bat didn't suspect a thing. Today, like other days, I had succeeded in smuggling a book past all the guards! And tomorrow would be another day.

The elevator finally arrived, and the robotic AI voice said, "The elevator has arrived. Please proceed in an orderly fashion. The doors will close in ten seconds. Nine, eight. . . ." Ugh, these machine voices really got on my nerves. I stepped into the elevator along with Dima, Baba, and a wave of other people, before our aerogel chamber prepared to glide along on the powerful nano-rod that would take us up.

If a media parachute ever flew up to me and asked about the happiest moments of my life, I wouldn't have to give it even a second's thought. I would look right at the parachute camera, flash a big smile, and say, without missing a beat, "Those thirty-eight seconds I spend on the elevator every morning, on my way to Quartzia."

CHAPTER 1

Every morning when I rode the elevator, I made a habit of looking toward the spot of light in the glass dome up top—the one that was pierced through by the rod. And, as the elevator capsule got closer and closer, I would imagine that this was my last trip on the elevator, and that the rest of my life would be up above, in Quartzia.

But would that dream ever come true?

2

The three of us left the elevator capsule and headed for Quartzia Square. Up ahead, a bird chased a butterfly through the spots of golden light that hung in the air. I felt a breeze so gentle it was like the brush of fingertips as it pushed my bangs off my forehead, and I gave my first smile of the day.

"We've got less than seven minutes to get to work," Dima said. "Hurry up."

By now, we were near the city's watchtower, which was called the Cedar Tree Building. It was a giant tower of see-through quartz that rose up through the clouds. Its lower floors held government offices, while the upper ones housed security. This was where Griffin bats went every day to sleep.

We had to get to the far side of the square to take the Barq pedestrian walkway that was near the Sea Wave Power Station. We hurried onto the platform. It was right by the station building, which was shaped like a giant mushroom. In the Comoros, we're surrounded by the ocean on all sides. To be honest, I really don't know how it's possible that all these thundering waves generate so little electricity for

CHAPTER 2

the Burrow that we're forced to live half of our life down there in darkness.

Dima and I helped Baba to one of the entrance points, where he jumped onto the lightning walkway, and we quickly hopped on behind him. Dozens of lightning walkways had been built by the Barq Company since I was little. They had spread out through the length and breadth of the city, chock-a-block with thousands of passengers.

"Without Barq, we would never get to work on time," Dima said.

"Without Barq," I said, "we could've saved up more than a quarter of our salaries."

"Yeah, but today we're really late."

"Oh, it's going to be fine," I told her. "Don't worry."

I noticed that the antennae were poking out of Dima's hair bun, so I pulled them out. These antennae were a pale imitation of the ones the Goldens wore, and they made us look nothing like them. Dima nudged me. "Hey. I spent a long time getting those right."

I ignored her and slipped them into my back pocket. After a minute, I felt her slip them out of my pocket and flick me across the back of the neck.

"Don't touch them again," she whispered, sticking her tongue out at me. But she didn't put them back in her hair—Dima and I hardly ever disagree.

Less than ten minutes later, we got to the giant blue sunflower that stood outside the door to the Museum of Modern Science, which we passed each day. We leapt off the walkway and hurried along the museum wall. The museum building was massive. It showcased Quartzia's scientific achievements, and one day I intended to visit it.

A golden-eyed man was walking near us with his young son, who also had golden eyes. These two were the only Goldens in a sea of Limiteds. I wondered what had drawn them out of their homes so early in the morning, since the Goldens usually slept in late. Unlike us Limiteds, the Goldens didn't start their workday until 10 a.m. Then they finished at 2 in the afternoon, which meant they went to work two hours after us and left two hours before us. Also, people with golden eyes earned many, many times our Limited wages. Father and son were both wearing turbo shoes, and they slowly lifted up above us.

A single pair of turbos cost 600 binar. All together, the three of us—me, Dima, and our dad—made 400 binar a month. The boy turned his shoes toward the lightning walkway, tugging his father by the arm, trying to get on the walkway. But his father stopped him, pulling him back. Lightning walkways were only for Limiteds like us.

"Why do they get to ride but not us?" the boy asked.

"They're different," his father said.

Different? What a polite way of putting it! It didn't begin to reflect the truth of who we were. We weren't just

CHAPTER 2

different, we were *lesser*. We were each categorized on one sad day when our mothers—or rather, our AI mothers—gave birth to us by registering our intelligence. Limiteds were anyone who got below the number 1111. My IQ number was 778, which meant 333 points separated me from happiness, a fact that nothing would ever change.

Now we sped up, racing to reach Professor Adam's house. When we got there, Baba held his forehead near the gate scanner, and it fired an electric pulse. Yasmina's voice rang out: "You are eight minutes and thirty-four seconds late." Yasmina was the house's virtual spirit. If you were ten minutes late, that meant a night in prison. A few times, we'd been more than ten minutes late, but Professor Adam had forgiven us.

Sometimes, Professor Adam would catch what I called the good-heartedness flu, but he would soon cure himself and go back to his old habits. This man, who was many years older than Baba, was strict and solemn, and we were all afraid of him. We started working for the professor soon after Mama died, after the sales from her paintings could no longer support us. It had been nine years since Mama's death. I had been seven years old.

Now, we walked through the gate and headed for the garden. Dima went straight to the greenhouse full of fruits and vegetables, while Baba and I headed for the main house. Fruits and veggies in their traditional shapes were rare in Quartzia, and anyone who wanted to eat them, the way Professor Adam did, had to grow them at home. His apples were round, and they were either red or yellow, with no other shapes or colors, and his eggplants were only long and black. When Professor Adam had seen me once with a bunch of blue apples I'd brought with me from the elevator plaza, he'd yanked them out of my hands and thrown them in the trash, saying, "Absolutely no genetically modified food in my home."

I hadn't even realized that blue apples were genetically modified until I'd seen the ones in his greenhouse.

Yet again, Baba held his forehead near a door scanner. This time, it was at the front of the quartz house. Here, Yasmina opened the door and said, in her monotone e-voice: "Come in quietly. Yesterday, the professor worked late in his lab. Today's breakfast will be a cheese and mushroom omelet at 8:20 a.m. Diyala must clean the library immediately, so that Professor Adam can take his breakfast in there."

Baba pulled his cooking coveralls from the sterilizer capsule and headed for the kitchen, while I took mine and went to the cleaning cart. In this house, Baba was the chef, Dima was the farmer, and I was the housekeeper. Welcome to the home of Professor Adam al-Azizi, head of Quartzia's Gene-editing Laboratory!

I pulled on my coveralls, drew up the zipper, and dragged the cleaning cart out of the closet. Then I climbed up onto the boarding platform and stood at the center while it brought me up to the second floor. For the zillionth time, I felt the book pressing against my waist. These books that

CHAPTER 2

I stole weren't going to fly off anywhere. So why couldn't I stop myself from constantly checking on them?

I stepped off the platform and walked down the bedroom hallway, where I could hear the sound of water running in the professor's Turkish bath. Every morning like clockwork, Professor Adam finished his workout on the machines and then went to bathe. I parked the cart next to the library door, since I'd have to return the book to its proper place before Professor Adam came out of the bathroom and stepped into the library. I asked the metacrystal disc on my wrist for the book's proper placement, and the phrase "9-23, left" popped into the air. I had to return the book to the ninth shelf and put it after the 22nd book, counting from the left. But . . . where was the ladder? I looked all around but couldn't find it. Strange!

I had put up with this stupid, non-automated ladder for years, and *now* it dared to disappear? Idiotic thing.

Nothing had changed in this library since the day I'd started working here. Several decades ago, the books here had been passed down to the Professor by his grandparents. And a hundred years before that, they had belonged to his grandfather's father. Many of the books here were made out of thin plates of actual tree cellulose called "pages," and machines had written on them with a black liquid called "ink."

In our time, books streamed one sentence after the next from our metacrystal discs, and paper books had gone totally extinct. So Professor Adam considered his books a treasure that must be carefully tended. Later, after he went to his lab, I'd have to borrow an extension arm from the garden and return the book to its proper place. Right now, I had to get the room ready for his breakfast. I turned on the vacuum mouse and put it on the ground, so that it started to suck up the dust, and I grabbed what Professor Adam called the "feather duster" and started to gently run it over all the books, the way he'd shown me.

One day, when I had forgotten to brush the dust off a book, Professor Adam had made me copy out a hundred pages from it. He gave me a liquid pen that had the word "Bic" written on it and told me to copy the words down on white cellulose pages. Professor Adam never tolerates mistakes. I don't even dare think, not even for a second, about what he'd do if he discovered I was taking his precious books with me down into the Burrow. Sometimes, the guards inside my brain wake up, and they force me to go home without a book. But when I can't get to the worlds I travel to in books, I feel so bored and lonely that the next day I hurry back, apologetic and ready to embrace those shelves.

After I put a quartz cleaning magnet on the library window, it started to squirt water, then wipe it off. Just then, I remembered that the library had no electric heat, and that I had to light the actual fire. I sprayed insulation gel on my hands and knees, so that they wouldn't get ashy, and the foam hardened immediately. I took the brush and got down on my knees, sweeping away the old ashes. Then

CHAPTER 2

I stacked up a few pieces of apricot wood in the fireplace, fired a hydrogen bullet at them, and the logs burst into flames. The fragrant smell of apricots wafted out.

Professor Adam used a real fire instead of an electric one because he's *traditional*. Sometimes I wondered: How could the head of the Quartzia Gene-editing Laboratory be so old-fashioned? I slid backwards on my knees, away from the fireplace, and started to straighten up. But then I bumped into something behind me, and it knocked me back down to my knees.

I turned and found Professor Adam standing there, his arms crossed. "Miss Diyala, I'm afraid I must search you. I believe you have been stealing my books!"

3

Professor Adam grabbed my arm and pulled me down the hallway into his office. My knees almost buckled beneath me. What was he going to do? When the door sensors were alerted to our approach, the door opened, and we stepped into the office. There, he let me go and wagged a finger in my face, saying, "Give me the book. Give it to me."

I stood in place, stiff as a stone. Should I hand it over? Had he really seen me do it? Should I deny it? Should I admit it? Would he hand me over to the Griffin bats? My lips trembled, and he reached his fingers toward the leg-pocket in my coveralls. Involuntarily, I jumped back from his hand. He gripped my wrist firmly, holding me in place as if I were a stake in the ground. What a Golden grip!

With his other hand, he reached toward the bulge on my waist and patted around until he found the book. "Take it out immediately," he ordered.

I turned around and unzipped the coveralls, lifted my shirt, and pulled out the book that had been tucked up against my waist. Then I zipped up, turned, and held it out to him. I didn't look him in the eye, but I knew his eyes would be boring into mine. He shouted to the house's spirit: "Yasmina, blow me up a sofa of solid smoke."

CHAPTER 3

"Yes, Sir," she answered in her monotone voice. The hissing sound of smoke spurted out, forming the shape of a sofa. He sat down on it while I stood facing him, paralyzed by terror and flooded with shame. I pushed my fingers into my bangs, which were tucked behind my ears, and tried to pull them down to cover my frightened eyes. As I did, I felt the slick of sweat on my forehead and realized that the foam gloves were still fixed to my palms, covered in ashes. I pulled off the gloves and tucked them in the pockets of my coveralls.

Professor Adam flipped through the book for a few seconds and then asked, "How long have you been stealing my books?" My brain said, *This is my first time*, but my tongue spoke first: "Five years."

Had my tongue lost its mind? Why was I getting myself into even deeper trouble?

On the wall behind Professor Adam, there was a painting of a deer caught in the headlights of one of those ancient cars that once ran on four wheels. In the last moment before the car hit it, horror filled the deer's eyes.

"Do your father and sister know about this?" he asked.

"No."

He smacked a hand against the book, and I jumped. "Tell the truth."

"I'm not lying," I said, my voice trembling. "They don't know. Do you really think Baba would've let me put myself in dange—"

"*Danger?*" he said, interrupting. "If you knew this was dangerous, then why did you do it? Because it's not just a danger to you, is it. It's a danger to whoever owns the books."

"I'm sorry that I put you in danger. Somehow, I'll get a gold card for the Quartzia library, and, from now on, I'll borrow my books from there."

He smacked his palms together. "Young lady, have you lost your mind? Don't you know that books are banned in the Burrow? Don't you know what the punishment is if you're found with one?"

I felt the tongues of fire that had been licking at my stomach rise up into my throat and burst out. "Goldens can't stop me from learning math and science! The only things they want me to know are how to make their food, clip their toenails, and clean their underwear."

Professor Adam's cheek muscles clenched so hard I could see them hug the bones. He paused a few seconds before he said, "Do you even know what you're saying? Have these words just sprouted off your tongue?"

I snapped back: "They've been stored up inside me for years. I—"

He cut in: "Don't you realize, you little fool, that if the bats catch you with a book, they'll kill you?"

"To me, a life without books is just a different kind of death."

CHAPTER 3

He stared at me for a long time. Minutes passed, and he sank into silent thought. Then, after what seemed like an eternity of silence, he finally said, "Well! It seems that you are fully aware of the ramifications of your thefts, and thus I am sure you're completely ready to face the consequences." Then he roared out, in a frightening voice, "Yasmina! Bring me Nabil and Dima."

"Yes, Master," Yasmina answered.

He was going to hand me over to the police—or to the Griffin bats! Was he calling in Baba and my sister so they could say goodbye? Poor Baba. This would be too hard on his health, and Dima was going to be crushed. My heart went crazy, pounding against my ribs. I heard the two of them approach, and then the doors opened. Baba's eyes asked me what was going on, but Professor Adam ended his confusion by saying, "Your daughter has been stealing my books for the last five years."

"I borrowed them," I said, over the professor. "I borrowed them and put them back. Count them if you don't believe me. You aren't missing a single book."

Baba's eyes were glued to the professor's lips, which said, "She'll need to face the consequences of her actions."

Dima turned to the professor. "Please, Professor Adam, please forgive her. She won't ever do it again. Don't hand her over to the Griffin bats—they'll kill her."

Baba got between me and Professor Adam. His back sheltered me, as though he wanted to protect me. I wished he really could! But what could a sickly man like Baba do when faced with a man like the professor, who had Golden muscles and genetically enhanced bones?

The professor rose from his invisible smoke couch and headed for an antique box in a corner of his office. A brass ring jutted out, stuck in a hole in the box. The ring made two turns, and then it let out a small *tick*. The ring and the hole are called a "lock" and a "key"—I heard about them once in an old movie, in the fourth-floor cinema inside the Burrow. The professor opened the lid of the box and took out a long stick that ended in a hook. "This is made from a plant called *bamboo*, which grew here in the Comoros two hundred years ago. My grandfather Aziz told me that they used to discipline thieves with this cane."

Then he waved the stick through the air several times, so that it made a *sweeeeeshhhh* sound that made the hairs on my arms stand on end. No one had ever hit me before. Was he going to hit me with that? I didn't want to be hit, but I didn't want to go to the bats, either, so . . . did I hope he was going to do it? Would he really? Baba waved his arms to get Professor Adam's attention, and then pointed at himself.

"Hit you? Of course I won't. You're a good man and you have stolen nothing. Anyhow, who said I would strike her with it? I was simply telling you what they used to do with thieves in the olden days." He laid the stick on his desk and went on: "When it comes to theft, Quartzian law is clear. The thief becomes the property of the one from

CHAPTER 3

whom they stole, and they serve him for free until they have paid off the full amount of their debt. Basically . . . the book that I'm holding in my hands, right now, costs at least two thousand binars, which means that you will be my possession for thirty months."

I gasped, as if I had just climbed a thousand steps. "I haven't stolen anything," I shouted. "I'm not going to become your possession for thirty months—or even thirty days! I would rather die than belong to someone."

He shrugged. "Listen, young lady. You do whatever you like. If you want me to hand you over to the police, then they'll appoint a lawyer to defend you in front of the judge. As you wish."

What would the judge rule when he discovered the book had been in the waistband of my pants? Would any judge rule in favor of a Limited against a Golden? I don't think it has happened, even once, in Quartzian history.

Professor Adam clapped his hands. "Should I tell Yasmina to call the police? Or do you agree that I will own you? You have to decide right now, since you have taken us all away from our work with your foolishness."

Baba turned and nodded, encouraging me to agree.

"You don't have a choice," Dima whispered. "No Limited in his right mind would go to the police of his own free will. You know what the police do to us. Just say yes. Say yes, and then we'll find a way out of this."

I hesitated, a voice inside me screaming, *Don't let anyone put a leash on you!* But the panic in Baba's eyes made me soften. He was afraid that Professor Adam would turn me over to the police if I refused. So I whispered in a rattling voice, "Yes."

"I didn't hear you," Professor Adam snapped.

"Okay!" I shouted, at the top of my lungs. "You own me."

"Yasmina," he said. "Find me the Ownership Collar."

In a chest of drawers set into the office wall, a small drawer with the number 132 on it opened. The professor stepped toward it, pulling out a copper collar that glowed with a small electronic light.

I knew these necklaces—you always saw them around the necks of people who were cleaning fish or out walking dogs. Their feet would drag along the ground, and their backs would be bowed with humility. Ownership Collars! Beneath me, our reflections on the titanium floor began to wobble. Tears flooded my eyes, so I pressed them shut with my fingers. Suddenly, I felt as though I were breathing through a thin straw.

The professor stood in front of me and reached out with the collar, his hands moving toward my neck, so I surrendered. I surrendered to him without bending. Then I looked to the side, so he couldn't see my eyes, and I saw that deer in the painting again: fragile, helpless, and surprised by death. On the glass of the painting's frame, I could see

CHAPTER 3

my own image reflected: my face stained with ashes from the fireplace, and my eyes wide with fear, defeated. . . and not at all golden. Oh, how I wanted those golden eyes.

I clutched my hands behind my back to stop myself from scratching out Professor Adam's stern eyes. A ringtone erupted from the necklace. A painful sensation travelled through my body, and then a mechanical voice stated: "The collar has been fastened. Only Professor Adam al-Azizi's fingerprint can unlock it."

Okay, so it really was true: It's pretty much impossible to get the necklace off without your owner's permission. But somehow, whatever it took, I would find a way to open it.

4

Stepping into my new room, I felt a chill run down my shoulders. "Yasmina," I said, "please heat the room up to 28 degrees." The numbers lit up on a display near the door. Professor Adam had announced that, from now on, this would be my room. He told Dima she could help me get it ready.

In Professor Adam's house, there were several spare bedrooms. I only ever went into this particular room once a month to clean it. Now, I threw myself down onto the smokefoam mattress; my knees were barely holding me up. I put an arm under my head and curled up tight. Dima lay down behind me on the mattress, hugging me and kissing the space between my shoulders. I had always wondered how all the indentured people we saw in Quartzia Square could accept the idea of being owned by someone else. Today, I had my answer. In Quartzia, there just wasn't much that separated you from becoming someone else's property. Read a book, and soon you'd finger a fire-colored copper chain around your neck.

Suddenly, as I lay on the mattress, the collar started to tighten, as if it wanted to strangle me. I sat up and took hold of it, trying to get it off, but it wouldn't budge. I tried to slip my fingers underneath it, but it gripped me even

CHAPTER 4

tighter. Its lock had settled into the gap in my collarbone, so I wrapped all ten fingers around it. But even though I pulled with all my strength, it just grew tighter and tighter. As I tugged, the collar fought back. I tried to get in at the clasp, but every link hugged the next and wouldn't move.

I felt it latch onto a lock of my hair. ENOUGH! I yanked at the strands and then stared at them, lying limp in my palm.

How had I let the professor put this thing around my neck? And what had stopped me from getting my nails under it? Goldens, bats, the government. And me. Every day, there had been a new kind of abuse, and every day I had been too cowardly to do anything about it.

Dima patted my shoulder and said, in a trembling voice, "Bismillah, bismillah." Maybe she thought I'd lost my mind. Maybe I *had* lost my mind. I hid my face in my arms and started to cry. I wasn't sure how much time passed like that, but when I opened my eyes, the sun that hung over the quartz windows had half-disappeared into the sea. I prayed it was all just a nightmare, but then my hands felt my neck, and I found that rotten collar still locked around my throat. Instead of lying on the smokefoam mattress, I sat up.

I found Baba and Dima sitting on chairs nearby, waiting for me to wake up. Dima came closer and sat down next to me. "We wanted to stay with you tonight, but you know . . . ." Limiteds were forbidden to be out in Quartzia at night; they all had to be back in the Burrow by sunset.

My sister put a hand on my knee and went on, "I cleaned the house for you today, and tomorrow I'll bring you your stuff."

She started to pull her hand away, but I clung to it like a little kid. Baba wrapped his arm around my shoulders and placed his free fingertips to his lips, a sign that I should eat.

"Baba made you crab with cloves and peppers, just the way you like it."

I kissed his palms and told him, "Don't worry, I'll eat." He already had so much weighing on his mind. Sadness was only going to make him sicker.

Dima took her sleeve and wiped my face with it. "You've got ash all over your face. In your hair, too."

I drew back, turning away from her sleeve. "I'll wash it off, don't worry."

Her hand was trembling. Ever since Mama's death, Dima hadn't had anyone but me. How was she going to last the next thirty months without me?

Baba pointed his thumb toward the door of the room, meaning he meant to say something about Professor Adam. Then he gave a thumbs-up with his other hand, showing that he thought the professor was a good man.

"If he was a good man, he would've forgiven me. We've been working for him ever since Mama died. That's nine whole years." When I said that, I felt like I was going to start crying all over again, but I got a hold of myself. I didn't

CHAPTER 4

want Baba to worry about me. He didn't know what to say, so instead of saying anything, he just hugged me.

"Go on," I said. "Leave now unless you want to spend the night in jail."

They nodded and left. I watched them cross the gardens and saw them stop for a few seconds near Professor Adam. Dima said a few words. She must have been asking permission to leave, but Baba stood to the side, not looking at Professor Adam. He had just surrendered his daughter to a man blinded by greed, and he hadn't been able to lift a finger to defend her. He must have been feeling totally helpless. But what could a poor, sick man like him do? It wasn't as if he had golden eyes.

Baba and Dima walked away from the gate, and I headed for the kitchen. I suddenly remembered that I hadn't eaten a single bite since yesterday, when we had eaten our lunch here before heading back to the Burrow. I walked into the kitchen and stepped toward the oven, saying, "Yasmina, I want a plate of food." A plate soon appeared in a slot at the center of the oven. After that, the oven's robot arm took a scoop from the pot that was in the oven, then dropped it onto the dish. I opened the oven door, took the plate, and sat down to eat. The meal must have been delicious, but on that day, everything tasted like dirt. The problem wasn't Baba's cooking—it was my tongue. I remembered that Baba used to make this same dish for Mama. He was a wonderful chef, and he didn't deserve this kind of treatment from Professor Adam.

Baba had prepared this amazing food, and Dima had grown all the ingredients. I had bought all the boxes and utensils on the shelves around me at the old souq, and I had cleaned them and put them in their places. Our fingerprints were on every single beautiful thing in this house, and we did all of the work here. Without us, this man's life would be miserable! The Goldens couldn't live for a single hour without the Limiteds. That's why, in the Burrow schools, the only thing they taught us was how to serve and pamper. I hated them so much!

On my wrist, the metacrystal disc buzzed, sending a shiver all through me. Yasmina said: "Professor Adam is waiting for you in the garden, near the statue of the dancing fish. This is the seventh ice statue from the—"

"Yasmina, enough," I cut in. "I know where he is, you windbag."

I counted out two seconds before her answer, and then synchronized my words with hers as she said, "There is no need for insults."

Whenever you said any kind of bad word, the stupid AI would say the exact same thing: *There is no need for insults.* Now, I ran my palms under the UV faucet until they were clean, and then I headed off toward the garden, fiddling with the metacrystal disc on my wrist. I switched the professor's call tone from buzz to chime. When this guy called for me, I didn't want my wrist to shake any more. I wanted to respond to him as calmly as I could.

5

I headed out into the gardens and walked down the path that was lined with ice sculptures of different animals. When I saw Professor Adam, I hurried up to him. "Yes, Professor?"

"Yes, *Master*," he said. "This is how you should address me from now on, as is appropriate to your new situation."

In your dreams, I thought.

He went on: "We need a notary to sign your ownership contract right away, so you can officially be my possession. You need to be indentured before the curfew, since the indentured are allowed to sleep in Quartzia."

Unfortunately, he was right. If my classification didn't change from Limited to Indentured before sunset, then the guards at the elevator checkpoint would notice I hadn't come back to the Burrow, and they would start looking for me.

Of course, he didn't wait for my answer. Instead, he said, "Yasmina, summon the notary immediately."

Seconds later, the metacrystal disc at his wrist projected a holographic image of a bald woman with a triangle drawn at the center of her forehead.

"I am the on-duty notary. How may I help you today?"

"I want to own this girl," he said.

My heart started to throb all over again. In a few minutes, it would be official. I would be an indentured servant in the eyes of the law and the people. I wished I could run, but I knew I wouldn't even get to the end of the street before the bats caught up with me.

"Name of the owner?" the bald woman asked.

"Adam al-Azizi."

The woman called up a virtual screen in front of her and said, "Date of birth?"

"January first, 2030."

It was now 2095, which meant Professor Adam was sixty-five years old. And I had thought he couldn't be a day over fifty!

The bald figure asked his profession, and he said, "Head of the Quartzia Gene-editing Laboratory."

The woman's expression changed. "We are honored to serve you, Professor Adam. I apologize for not recognizing you from the start. I don't know what's wrong with me. It's been a tiring day. I have—"

"It's fine," the professor interrupted. "I too have had a tiring day. So let's get on with it!"

CHAPTER 5

Then he gave me an angry look. Oh, this wicked old book-lover. How unlucky he was! How tiring it must be to be waited on hand and foot all day long!

A blue light flashed out from the bald figure, shooting over the professor's face. Then an electronic voice said, "Professor Adam al-Azizi. Pupils and face identified." Then the notary turned to me and asked, "Indentured's name?"

The word *indentured* stuck in my throat, and I couldn't speak. Professor Adam answered for me: "Diyala Karthala." I almost added my date of birth, but he said it without asking me: "September 9, 2079." Had he remembered all that from the day he'd hired me? That was nine years ago! I had been seven years old, and back then, the cleaning cart had been too heavy for me to push. Did Goldens have extraordinary memories? The bald figure recorded the information and then asked about my job.

"Housekeeper," the professor answered.

"One question remains," she said. "That is, the reason for indenture."

Would he tell her that I was a thief? That wouldn't be fair! That one word would haunt me for the rest of my life. If he said it, no one would hire me ever again.

"A debt Diyala was unable to pay," he said.

I heaved out a sigh of relief. Debt was better than theft. He was a wicked old book-lover, but a gentleman, too.

Maybe I should take the opportunity to slather myself in some of that nobility oozing off him?

"How much debt?" the woman asked. "And how long is the period of indenture?"

Were her questions ever going to end? Her hair was going to grow back before we were finished.

"Two thousand binar," he said. "Thus, I will own her for thirty months."

Two thousand binar was the cost of one shelf in this man's shoe cabinet. What would he lose if he pardoned me? But the blue light scanned my forehead, and my identity was confirmed. My identity, which was defined by my intelligence, which was less than 1111.

After that, the notary said: "The period of your contract has been set to thirty months. She has been moved from the category of Limited to Indentured. Congratulations!"

Congratulations on your indenture? What a way to sugarcoat death. The woman asked Professor Adam if he needed her for anything else, and he thanked her and said no. After that, she leapt back into the disc on his wrist, from which she'd appeared a few minutes ago, and vanished.

He turned to me. "Now that it's official, there are a few things you need to understand."

I wasn't ready to understand anything, but he went on: "As I'm sure you realize, those who are indentured are not

CHAPTER 5

paid for their work. So, starting from today and until the end of your contract, you will not receive any wages."

"How would I know anything about the salaries of the indentured? Up until a few hours ago, I was a free person, you—"

"Well," he said, stepping on my words. "That has changed now, has it not? And you are the one who has brought about this new arrangement."

I went silent. He was the one who had brought about this new arrangement, not me. He was the one who'd decided not to forgive. And now I understood why he had done it—in order to avoid paying my salary! What an old miser.

"Currently," he went on, "your range of movement is limited to this house and the walkway around—"

"Why risk it?" I interrupted. "Why not stop me at the gate? Then you'd be sure I could never run away, right?"

He smiled. "Say, 'Why risk it, *Master*.' I won't punish you for forgetting the word this time, nor will I punish you for interrupting. But I warn you that I am not often so forgiving."

Tell me something I don't know! As if I didn't know he wasn't forgiving! If he had one iota of forgiveness in his body, I wouldn't be here tonight. After pressing the disc at his wrist several times, he said, "I've adjusted your range. Now you can go all the way to the old market. But one step more, and the collar will paralyze you. And believe you me, it is not a pleasant experience."

I knew about the paralyzing convulsions that the collar caused any indentured person who went outside their allowed range. I'd seen it once, with my own eyes. A poor indentured child had accidentally gone outside his range, and the collar struck him like a thunderbolt, so that he fell to the ground shuddering, unable to move. Professor Adam always sent me to the old market to get groceries and cleaning supplies, because the stuff there was GMO- and chemical-free. I knew that he'd put the old market in my range because it didn't offer crowbot delivery service, like the other, newer markets.

"You will have a radius of 79 meters, centered on this house. That means you will have a total area of movement of . . ." The professor knotted his fingers together. "Yasmina, what is the area of a circle with a radius of 79 meters?"

Before Yasmina could answer, I did: "19606.68 square meters."

Two seconds later, Yasmina said, "19606.68 square meters, Master."

The professor looked at me in astonishment, as though his grandfather had just leapt out of the grave. Oh, how shocking it was, to know that some of us Limiteds also had a brain inside our skull as an added bonus.

CHAPTER 5

"Have they added math to the curriculum at the Burrow schools?"

I could hear sincere confusion in his tone, and I answered him with a challenge: "Or maybe I read about the subject in an interesting math book I borrowed when its owner was away?"

His tone sharpened. "'Maybe I read about the subject in an interesting math book I borrowed when its owner was away, *Master.*' That is what you should have said. This word, Master, will help you get used to your new circumstances. The penalty for forgetting is that you will start work tomorrow at five in the morning. And you will start your day by cleaning the walk-in freezer. Now, go shower and sleep. Your face and clothes are covered in ash. You'll find clean clothes in the silicone capsule in your room. Is that clear?"

I suddenly remembered that I hadn't let Dima clean off my face. I wished I had. "It's clear . . ."

The professor turned toward me and fixed his eyes on mine, as if waiting for something, so I added, "Mas. . . ter."

Had I not said it, he probably would have made me wake up before dawn. He stood up and walked over to the house, leaving me standing in the garden, a miserable ashy statue among all the gleaming ones. I felt slapped in the face by all of it: *You are mine,* and *Call me Master,* and *No salary for you,* and, *Your world is now 19.5 square kilometers.* Yes, we

Limiteds might lack intelligence, but the Goldens lack a much more important organ: the heart!

Plus, I thought, *nobody owns me. Even if I said the word Master a thousand times, I would not forget that no one is my master except me.*

I wasn't going to work for anyone who refused to pay me. Soon, I would fly off, free as a butterfly. Soon, I would take off this collar and the bald notary would change my category listing to: Runaway.

6

The bathtub stood at the center of the room, looking like half of a crystal ball. I stepped into the middle of it and water fell from a cloud that hung above my head, near the ceiling. The water smelled like oranges, but it was a shade of azure blue. I looked at the chrome mesh beneath my feet and saw black water running down the drain. Had that fireplace sneezed out a whole bag of ash on me? I pressed the button for a shampoo, and the water changed color. My hair was foamy for a while before the water ran clear. And when I stepped out of the tub, the water stopped immediately.

I took a towel out of a drawer beneath the sink and wrapped it around me before I walked to the silicon capsule in the corner. I took out a dress decorated with yellow roses, running my fingers over its soft fabric. It was Pictipote silk, one of the Comoros's most valuable products, and one they exported to countries all around the world. Here in the Comoros, scientists had isolated the spider's fibron genes, linking them to a nucleic thread of bacteria, and after that, the spiders had begun to spin like crazy. It was an abundant resource, as strong as it was soft.

This dress had a short sash around the shoulders. All my life, I've hated the Golden girls' Pictipote silk dresses with their long, dangling scarves. But today a strange feeling welled up as I put it on. It was a mix of nostalgia and sadness that I couldn't understand. Then I found a comb with two letters stamped on it: AA. Was it for Adam al-Azizi? Or someone else? I combed out my hair with it, and I found the comb was gentle with my tangles. Yet the comb, the tub, the clothes, and all the other things in the room didn't make me any less lonely.

I threw myself down onto the mattress of solid smoke. I slept so fitfully that, if it wasn't for the nightmares, I would have thought I hadn't slept at all. I dreamed about the Burrow, and the Griffin bats, and . . . Mama!

When I woke up, my pillow was wet. I didn't know if it was because my hair had still been wet from last night's shower, or because I'd been crying. The watch on my wrist said it was 4:56 a.m., which meant I had to be in the kitchen in four minutes if I wanted to avoid the professor's temper. If I was late, that snitch Yasmina would tell him. I quickly tied my hair behind my head and hurried to the kitchen. I put on the snowsuit I usually wore when cleaning the refrigerator, and then pulled on a protective mask. The suit wouldn't keep the cold out for more than half an hour, so I had to work fast. I pulled on the hydraulic sleeves that helped me carry heavy food items, dragged out the cleaning cart, and then stepped into the walk-in fridge.

On the walls around me, endless shelves were crammed with meat, vegetables, and more. I had no idea why this man packed his walk-in fridge with so many traditional foods when the rest of the world was filled with engineered ones

CHAPTER 6

that were cheaper, better-tasting, and in lots of different shapes and colors. I'd always hated cleaning this room. My breath steamed up the glass of my mask, and I had to keep wiping it off. The icy vapor stung my ears. With the help of the hydraulic sleeves, I pulled down all the items that were on the shelves and stacked them up on the floor. The mopping snails cleaned the shelves while I wiped down the food containers and put them back in their places. In addition to the meat and vegetables, there were lots of clear plastic bags with labels like "California locusts," "elephant mosquitoes," and "mountain flies." Each of these bags held an insect the size of a watermelon. If a mosquito that big bit me, it would drink a half a liter of my blood!

I knew Professor Adam didn't eat insects. So . . . did he keep them for his research?

Despite my protective suit, I felt frost creeping into my bones, so I stepped out of the walk-in fridge. I decided to leave Round Two until after I'd drunk something warm. I went out and was surprised to see Dima and Baba coming in through the kitchen door. I glanced down at my wrist and saw it was only 6:12 in the morning. Dima gave me a hug and said, "We missed you, so we came early to check on you."

I missed them more. I'm not good with emotions, but I didn't want Dima to pull away. Her arms were warm, and they quieted my chattering teeth. I rested my head on her shoulder for a few moments, and she whispered, "My ears are relieved to have your advice back." And I said, "And mine are relieved to have your babbling."

Baba joined us, throwing his arms around the both of us. I glanced at our reflection in the glass door; we looked like a group of penguins I'd once seen in an encyclopedia. Penguins used the body heat of the group to stay warm in the face of snowstorms. And like us, penguins were stuck in the arctic desert, battered by harsh weather.

Suddenly, Professor Adam's voice made us all jump. He was standing at the kitchen door, and he gazed at us for a few seconds before he said, "Dima, please go pick some fresh fruit for us, and Nabil, please prepare breakfast for two. That is, of course, if the International Hugging Symposium has come to an end."

I hated this man.

"Yes, Professor Adam," Dima and Baba answered.

The protective suit I was wearing clearly reminded him of my punishment, and he asked me, "Have you finished cleaning the cold storage?"

"I've finished most of it, and I'll do the rest now."

He stared at me, waiting for me to finish my sentence with the word *master,* but it got stuck in my throat. I wasn't going to be able to say it in front of Baba and Dima. It would make them feel even sadder.

When I gave up on saying that word, he said, his eyes heavy with meaning, "You'll bring us breakfast in the laboratory."

CHAPTER 6

"Understood," I said, forgetting once again to say the word this arrogant man's ears so loved. I didn't think he would ask me to clean the refrigerator a second time. So what punishments would his pompous brain come up with next? He didn't leave me guessing for long. His words projected up from the metacrystal disc at my wrist: "You will clean the library shelves in Locker Number One for the next two days: today and tomorrow. And this time, the use of hydraulic sleeves is forbidden."

I swiped my palm through the air in front of me, and the words disappeared. This wouldn't be a serious punishment. First, because I was missing books. And second, because I would use the hydraulic sleeves anyway, and he'd never even notice.

When Baba had finished preparing the food, I took off my protective suit so I could carry it to the laboratory. Once I had the suit off, Dima saw my clothes and whistled in admiration. She ran a hand over the dress and asked, "Where did you get that? It's so soft! And it looks cute on you!"

When would this girl's mind grow up?

"Open the capsule in my room and take whatever clothes you want," I said.

Her eyes sparkled, and then she leaned forward and hugged me, showering me with kisses. "I'm going to look more beautiful than gold."

I pulled back and tapped a forefinger against her forehead. "The gold is in here. In your head!"

She said nothing, but I knew that—as usual—she was inwardly laughing at me.

Next, I guided the flying food tray toward the laboratory. As expected, bars of red light blocked me from opening his door.

"Yasmina, please let me in," I said.

"All right," she answered.

Then I waited. And I waited. The lab was one of the places that we were forbidden to enter. Only Professor Adam could go in here. Over the years, he had given us clear warnings not to go anywhere near it, and none of us had dared step inside before this. Two whole minutes passed before the bars disappeared and I was able to open the door.

I expected to find the professor standing beside the door, waiting to take the tray from me, but I didn't see anyone. This meant I had to go all the way in and deliver the food. I piloted the tray of food between the tubes and machines that made soft buzzing sounds as their lights flashed on and off.

I could hear Professor Adam's voice, and the voice of someone else, coming from near the quartz wall, and I headed toward them. I found the professor with a guest: a young man with dark skin, cute dimples, and lips the color

CHAPTER 6

of apricots. The young man got up when he saw me. "Hi," he said. "I'm Raji, the professor's assistant."

Had he really stood up out of *respect* and *talked to me?* Couldn't he see the color of my eyes? Was his eyesight weak? Well, he must be kicking himself now. Or maybe, I thought, he's a Limited like me? But no, I had made no mistake about the color of his eyes: they were as golden as clove honey.

"Hello, Raji-the-professor's-assistant." I set the flying breakfast tray down between them. I was about to leave when Professor Adam said, "Wait."

So I stood there. What did he want now?

The professor walked up to a cocoon-like glass coffin that had wires sprouting from it. "Lie down here."

I stiffened like the pillar of blue bioluminescence that stood behind them. "So, what, I've been promoted from slave to lab rat now?"

"Would you prefer that I grab you and throw you in the machine?"

The professor took a step forward, but Raji interjected: "The professor just wants to make sure that anyone living in the house is free from common diseases."

I swallowed, giving myself a few seconds to calm down so that I wouldn't bite the professor's head clean off his body. "You seem to have forgotten that this girl, the one you're so afraid might have a *common disease*, is the same one who's been bringing you your food all these years."

In a fury, the professor lifted both arms and shook an index finger at me, clearly intending to spit out some new punishment. But Raji spoke first: "Please, Miss Diyala. You won't feel a thing. The professor's only going to take your pulse and check a few of your vitals."

This was the first time I'd heard the word *miss* uttered by anyone with two golden eyes. My legs took me immediately to the coffin without waiting for my approval, and I found myself lying contentedly on its hard surface.

"I'm also going to put a helmet and glasses on you," Raji whispered. "The glasses will project a series of images. Try not to close your eyes. If you do, I'll tap your hand with my fingers to remind you to open them again. Ok?"

What do *a series of images* have to do with any common disease? But I nodded, so he pulled out a helmet that had all sorts of antennae sticking out of it and fitted it over my head, and then he put glasses over my eyes. Cold metal cuffs encircled my wrists and ankles, stabilizing my arms and legs. After a moment, I heard a faint sound coming from the helmet, and the glasses began to flash images that were hard to grasp. The rapid-fire flashes hurt my eyes, so I closed them and hummed a tune my mother used to sing to me. Then I felt Raji's warm fingertips tapping the back of my hand. I remembered that he'd asked me not to close my eyes, so I opened them again, and they stayed like that for a

CHAPTER 6

few moments. But then I'd forget and close my eyes again, and Raji would pat my hand, and I'd open them.

After a while, the noises and flashes stopped. They took off my helmet and glasses and loosened the metal cuffs. Raji helped me sit up. I felt ok, just a little dizzy.

"All right," Professor Adam said. "Leave now, and I'll ask for you when I need something."

I wanted to ask what had just happened, but I knew no one would tell me.

"Thank you," Raji said, and I gave him a smile. Then I made my way through the machines, back to the door. I asked Yasmina to open it, and she did. But before I left, I waited there for a moment, listening. "How much?" Raji's voice asked. "Six," Professor Adam replied.

Six what? Did I have some disease that would kill me in six months? Maybe I had six diseases? But I didn't feel any symptoms! Maybe I should smash six machines in that laboratory so that this condescending professor would stop treating me like a lab rat.

But once again, I hadn't broken anything, and I didn't have an answer!

7

When I got back to the kitchen, I found Dima had finished cleaning the walk-in fridge. If Professor Adam found out about it, he'd be furious. That made me smile. Although he usually didn't get angry with Dima. He'd just get angry with me.

Baba tugged my shoulder before he set down a flying tray that had three dishes full of a delicious breakfast: Fragrance-free sheep's cheese; tea made from the leaves of some plant, the name of which I didn't know; hot bread; and apricots that had one red cheek and one orange one. I smiled when I saw these apricots, which reminded me of Raji's lips.

"Professor Adam has a young man with him now. Someone named Raji," I said. "Do you know him?"

Dima nudged my shoe with hers and said, "Abu Al-Ghamaztayn? He's a musician. But he doesn't use electronic instruments. He plays on some kind of wooden box that has strings tied to it. Usually, you go into the laboratory through the garden door, so you wouldn't see him. But I can see him from the greenhouse. He's been here a few times. He helps the professor with his research."

CHAPTER 7

"Does he rest the wooden box against his legs when he plays? Or does he hold it against his shoulder?"

I'd read about two different musical instruments, one called the oud and the other the violin, and I really wished I could hear what they sounded like! Dima had never read anything other than schoolbooks and ads for beauty products. Whenever she saw me reading, she asked why I bothered. But reading increased my knowledge. And as my knowledge grew, I felt stronger, even with this collar around my neck!

"He rests it against his legs," Dima said.

So he was an oud player, then. But what was a musician doing in a laboratory for genetic cloning? That's what I needed to find out. Baba motioned for me to eat, so I took a bite of my bread and cheese. They were as tasty as I'd hoped. I threaded my fingers between Baba's and kissed the back of his hand. He kissed mine, too. Then he used a finger to trace a smile over my lips. I smiled. He raised his hands and pointed at the sky, and I said, "Ameen." He must have been praying that I would be free again soon. I was glad that God could hear the voice of the heart.

We finished eating, and Baba put all the plates into the UV sterilizer. As I stared at the plates, Dima poked me and whispered, "Didn't you see Raji's golden eyes? Are you stupid?"

But that's not what was on my mind. Instead, I was mulling over an idea that had come to me in one of my nightmares, about how to get rid of this cursed collar. I whispered to my sister, "Dima, do you remember that old man, Daddy Three Arms? I want you to go tell him that he's got to find a way to disable this collar and help me escape. Ask him how much it will cost."

Dima's eyes widened with fear. "Are you going to run away?"

"You know me. Do you really think I'm going to last like this?"

For a long moment, she was silent. Then she closed her eyes and slowly nodded. God only knows what she was thinking. "How are you going to get the money to pay him?"

"I'll steal money from here. The professor already thinks I'm a thief—so let me steal!"

Dima gasped, so I put a hand over her mouth and whispered, "I'm going to run away from this country, and then I'll send for you guys."

She pulled my hand off her mouth. "You're crazy!"

She stalked away without giving me an answer. She didn't believe that I really could leave this country, then bring her and Baba to live with me. But even if she didn't believe me, she'd do what I asked. She always did.

After breakfast, I went to the library to finish my punishment. It wasn't easy to get down all those books without hydraulic sleeves. I tried to use them, but the sleeves were loud. I thought Yasmina would hear them and

CHAPTER 7

snitch to the professor, so I took them off right away. Less than two hours into the job, my elbow muscles spasmed. Would Professor Adam notice if I quietly asked Dima to help me? I looked out the window, searching for Dima, and I saw her in the distance, walking around the farm in her new clothes. The sun made her look even brighter. She was wearing a berry-purple dress as she filled the basket she was carrying. No one on earth was prettier than Dima.

When our mother died, Dima was five and I was seven. All I remember about that day was the boys who danced in the courtyard around the elevator at night, saying, "That's the painter's daughter. She doesn't look so good." Then I remember them stopping their dance and escorting me back to the apartment. Of course, Mama wasn't there anymore. I knew she was dead, but *how* did I know? I still wasn't sure!

From that day on, I felt it was my responsibility to protect Dima. She made a thousand little problems for herself because of how careless she was at school and in the Burrow, but I never let anything happen to her. I was terrified a day would come when the professor would punish her, so I had to confront him first. But so far, that day hadn't come—he never punished her, even though she sometimes made mistakes. Punishments were for me alone. I didn't understand what it was about me that made this man so angry.

Now, I decided to rest for a few minutes, massage my sore muscles, and then get back to it. I threw myself down on a chair. The metacrystal disc on my wrist flashed: "In five minutes, the Quartzia Competition for Academic Excellence will begin." I clapped a hand against my forehead. After all the terrible things that had happened these last two days, I'd almost forgotten it was time to tune into my favorite program. This season, the Quartzia competition would focus on math questions. I was sure it was going to be a great season.

"Yasmina," I said. "Show me the Quartzia Competition for Academic Excellence."

A moment later, the laser projector that hung on the library ceiling shot out a holographic projection of the competition studio, so that it looked like the studio was at the center of the library. I was afraid the professor might catch me watching the competitions, so I told Yasmina, "Turn down the volume, you idiot. Fast."

"There is no need for insults," she said.

I had followed all the seasons of the Quartzia competitions so far. The host's name was Manar Sikmadar, and he was a mathematician whose ancestors had been scientists just like him. In the last few years, the seasons had focused on physics, chemistry, genetics, programming, and other sciences in which the Comoros excelled. There were three stages. In each stage, Sikmadar asked questions, and the first contestant to answer would advance to the next, more difficult stage.

CHAPTER 7

The first two stages were held in a virtual theater, but the final elimination round was in the Quartzia City Stadium, and of course everyone in the city attended. Now, a virtual doorman welcomed me in through a rectangle of light near the studio gate. "No. 2114442," he said. "Welcome to the brilliant Quartzia competition. Please design an avatar to your liking to represent you here in the studio. Your seat is No. 455. When you finish designing your avatar, your control armor will appear."

No. 2114442? That must be the ID number that belonged to the laser projector on the ceiling. The laser projector, of course, was registered to Professor Adam, a resident of Quartzia, which explained why I had been given the doorman option. This gave me the chance to participate and choose an avatar to represent me in the studio.

A smile crept over my lips. Down in the Burrow, we didn't have a chance to choose an avatar to represent us in the theater, much less to participate in the competition! We just watched them passively, without interacting in any way. This year's season was going to be a lot more fun!

The avatar I chose was a thin, short man with hair that looked like Albert Einstein's. He wore those glass circles over his eyes that scientists had used a century ago. I called him Einstein and pressed the "complete" button. After that, words appeared in the air: "Mr. 2114442, we would like to inform you that, due to the serious nature of these competitions, if you participate in today's match and are chosen to advance to the next round, then you will not be able to withdraw from the competition. If you do withdraw, you will be subject to legal penalties, including criminal charges. Are you certain you want to compete?

These words disappeared, replaced by the words "agree" and "decline," which hung in front of me in the air.

I wanted to compete so badly! When the security forces investigated the competitors, as they usually investigated everything, they would find out that Professor Adam was the owner of No. 2114442. No one would ever suspect that a *woman* in his house was competing instead of him. Although let's say I did escape with Daddy Three Arms before the second round, and the security forces summoned the professor after he missed the second round. When they investigated his absence, they'd be convinced that he wasn't the one who withdrew from the competition. Instead, it had been his escaped property. They would never bother him about that. After all, the security forces treated the Goldens with respect.

Ahhhh I wanted to participate so badly! I'd always wondered whether all those long hours spent solving math problems had put me on the same level as the Goldens. Now was finally my chance to find out. I pressed the "agree" button, and blue laser armor and a helmet appeared in front of me with the words "control armor" written beneath it. I put it on and started moving my arms and legs. Einstein imitated me.

CHAPTER 7

There was an empty seat in the middle of the fourth row, Number 55, which must have been reserved for Einstein. So I moved until Einstein got to his chair and sat down.

Sikmadar had just started the competition with a question I didn't understand. One of the avatars hunched up on a chair was the first to answer. This person looked like a dinosaur. Sikmadar walked up to that avatar and said, "Mr. Dinosaur of the Sea is the first to give the correct answer. Congratulations, you will be joining us in the second round."

The audience applauded enthusiastically. I'd have only a minute before he asked the second question. I took off my armor and hurried to the library door. I poked my head out into the corridor to see whether Professor Adam had left his laboratory. To my relief, I saw that the red bars of light were still shielding the lab's door. Was Raji still in there, too?

I hurried back before I missed the second question. When I got back, I found a popcorn vendor trying to sell Einstein a bag of hot popcorn. I finished putting on my helmet and armor and said, "Buzz off." Einstein's lips moved with the words "buzz off" and the salesman walked away. I sat quietly, listening carefully for the next question. Manar Sikmadar said, "What do the following numbers equal: 1 + 2 + 3 + 4 + 5 + 6, and so on until 1000?"

Without even realizing it, I moved the laser arm and made Einstein slam down on the button in front of him.

Sikmadar walked up to Einstein and said, "You didn't even give it a moment's thought, Mr. Einstein! I hope your answer is correct."

"The answer is 500," I said.

Sikmadar raised his arms into the air and called out, "Aaamaaazing! Congratulations, Mr. Einstein, you will be joining us in the second round. Please join the competitors' bracket to find out who will be lucky enough to join you."

I moved the laser armor until I'd guided Einstein to the competitors' bracket. But just then, Yasmina's voice rang out, asking me to take the professor his lunch, so I jumped up and rushed toward the door. I'd have to take the food to the lab and hurry back to see the end of the competition.

8

Ever since Mr. Einstein—that is, ever since I qualified for the second round of the Quartzia competition a few days ago—I've had the taste of sweetness under my tongue. These arrogant people claim that they're better at science than everyone else, but it turns out that even an indentured girl like me knows more than they do. My self-confidence blossomed, and I was happy, even though I didn't dare tell anyone about it. If I told my father, he'd scold me, thinking that I had broken some law. And with Dima, I couldn't be sure she'd keep it a secret.

Another thing that made me feel optimistic was that Dima had told Daddy Three Arms that he had to smuggle me out, and he'd promised to do it within the next week. So I wouldn't be trapped here much longer. All I had to do now was find a spot in this house where the professor had stashed a lot of money, which I could use to pay Daddy Three Arms.

Lately, the professor had changed his punishments from cleaning the library shelves to searching through its books for the solutions to puzzles he gave me to solve. These puzzles weren't easy. Each time, I had to read through several books to find the answer. Yesterday, I wasn't in the mood to search through the professor's books, so I didn't find the solution to his riddle. I expected him to punish me by increasing the number of puzzles he gave me the next day, but instead, the tyrant made me stand facing the wall for an entire hour without moving, as if I were a little kid in the Burrow school, while he sat next to me, reading a book and sipping the juice my father had made for him. I felt sick at the idea that Raji would see me like this.

When evening fell, I watched Dima and Baba leave before it got dark. Dima had put her new clothes into the vacuum packer and then crammed them into a small tin cylinder that she tucked into her belt pocket. Every day, she took a few items of clothing out of my closet and left here with them, as though she were carrying out a million binar. She couldn't take it all at once, or the guards at the elevator would suspect that she was carrying stolen goods. In the pockets of Baba's belt, there were other cylinders full of lunch pills. They were originally turkey and peas, but we'd put them into a device that sucked out the liquid and turned them into tablets. This way, the residents of Apartment 880 could add water to these tiny tablets, heat them up, and enjoy a delicious meal.

Apartment 880 belongs to our neighbor Kawthar, who lost her hand because she worked for a crocodile breeder who was supposed to sell them as pets after the company that cloned them added in a few rabbit genes to the mix. Although, from her loss of a limb, I guessed that this cloning company was a fraud. Either way, the result was an unemployed mother and four children.

CHAPTER 8

After they had left, the metacrystal disc on my wrist buzzed, and the professor's voice emerged: "Diyala, come to my office."

I raced over, and he said, "In the refrigerator, you'll find insects in bags in—"

I interrupted: "I know where they are." Then I remembered the ache in my arms from carrying all those library books. Fearing a new punishment, I added, "Sir."

"I am expecting important visitors from the Griffin bats," he said.

I grew more attentive as soon as I heard those two words, "Griffin bats." This meant there was no room for error. I nodded obediently, and he went on, "I want you to heat up twenty of the insects for them. Put them in the oven, and when it dings—"

"I know how to use the oven . . . Sir!"

"In the basement, you will also find bottles labeled 'Aged Deer Blood.' Choose three of these bottles from the cabinet labeled 2080 and put them in the cooling machine before you serve them."

"Understood."

"Take care, as I will not tolerate any mistakes today."

As if he tolerated mistakes any day.

"And the cups?" I asked.

"We won't need cups or plates," he said. "Just put the items directly on the tray. Now go."

Then he said, "Yasmina, let me know when the Griffin bats arrive."

"Yes, Sir," she replied.

Finally, I had learned the secret of all the insects that were in the walk-in fridge. The bats must come here often. And they must come at night, after we had usually gone home. But what brought them out here? Well, I'd find out later today, when they arrived. I raced to the kitchen, took the disgusting bugs out of the walk-in fridge, put on my foam mitts, and pulled the insects out of their bags. I felt sick at the sight of them and had to close my eyes. But it was even worse when I'd closed my eyes—I imagined those horrible bats devouring the insects with their hideous mouths, which were hidden among the wrinkles of their peeling faces. My stomach churned.

Yasmina's voice rang out, and I flinched.

"The Griffin bats have arrived," she said.

They were here! Through the wall of quartz, I could see Professor Adam greet them at the garden gate and motion for them to enter. There were three Griffin bats. They weren't wearing armor or carrying whips, like the ones we were used to seeing down in the Burrow. Instead, they were wearing short shirts, belted at the waist, that barely came down to their knees. Their legs were rough and thin,

CHAPTER 8

covered with hair, and their shoulders were decorated with ylang-ylang flowers. Did that mean these were generals?

A shiver ran through my body, and I felt the collar bite even deeper into my neck. The three Griffin bats were joined by a woman with golden eyes and hair that looked like a river of silver. Her clothes were golden, too—which meant she was a top government official, since they were the only ones who wore that color. *Who are you?* I wondered. The professor led them to his office. After that, his commanding voice boomed up from my wrist: "In addition to the insects, I require slices of monkey brain with lemon. You'll need to bake it in the oven with the insects. Is that clear? And a cup of pasteurized milk, too."

"Yes, Sir," I answered.

I hurried into the walk-in refrigerator, where I asked, "Yasmina, where is the monkey brain?"

A moment later, the compartment where the brain was located lit up, and I pulled it out. I put the insects and brains in the oven, and Yasmina told me, "Seventeen kilos and two hundred grams. That means it will be ready in 76 seconds."

I asked Yasmina to open the basement door and hurried down. She turned on the lights for me even before I asked her to. Her stupidity was improving every day. She must have been infected by my intelligence.

Down in the basement, wooden shelves lined the walls, and each shelf was filled with vials—there was nothing else. How many bats were coming here every year for the professor to need such a huge supply of blood? I heard a faint roaring sound coming from the center of the cellar and spotted exhaust vents. Those vents must be sucking up dust, which was why Professor Adam never asked me to clean the basement. I picked up the vials filled with their disgusting contents and, on my way out, saw a giant box with the letters AA etched onto it. Just like the letters on the comb! I was about to set down the bottles so I could give it a closer look when Yasmina's unpleasant voice rang out: "The food is ready. Open the oven door."

I remembered the professor's threat that he wouldn't tolerate any mistakes, and so I raced up to take out the gooey insects before they became smoky insects. The box wasn't going to run away, and I could take my time looking through it later. Now, I set the food and vials of blood onto a flying tray and guided them toward the office.

I whispered to Yasmina that she should let the professor know that I was at the door. I hoped he would just come out here and carry the tray inside himself, but he didn't. Instead, the door opened. Yasmina's voice told me, "Come in."

I entered and found Professor Adam and the woman sitting alone on two couches of solid smoke. Where had the bats gone?

Just then, a sticky trail of white liquid dripped from the ceiling and fell with a splat on the floor. It landed just a

CHAPTER 8

step away from me. I looked up and found the bats hanging upside down from the arms of the high chandeliers, saliva dribbling from their mouths. There was a lot of gossip down in the Burrow about how poisonous that saliva was. I tried to steady my trembling steps as I carefully shepherded the flying tray along in front of me. These antique chandeliers were a hundred years old, and Professor Adam made me clean them with a piece of cloth made from a plant called "cotton," which I was only allowed to dampen with plain water. I was sure that he was boiling with anger inside at those bats hanging from the chandeliers.

Then, in the blink of an eye, the food and drink disappeared from the flying tray. I almost screamed, but I choked it back at the last moment. I watched the bats warily as they settled on the couches and ate their food. The insects disappeared in one bite, and the bottles were emptied with a single gulp. The sounds of the locusts' bodies crunching between their teeth made my bones ache. Why did these creatures scare me so much?

I glanced over at the professor and saw him scolding me with his eyes. Then I realized that my fear of the bats had paralyzed me so much that I'd forgotten all about the woman. I hurried toward her with the brains and the cup of milk, bowing low so she could take them from me.

But she ignored me and said, "Oh Adam, do you really still remember my favorite dish and drink?"

He smiled. "Of course, my dear lady." But I felt from his smile and his tone that he was really saying, *Of course, my hideous sorceress.*

I stayed bent over, and she ignored me. She didn't seem to be in any hurry. It might be summer before she took this disgusting dish from my hand. I didn't know what to do—should I stand up? Should I stay bent over like this? Should I smack her in the head with the plate of brains, so that there would be two brains on the plate instead of one?

The professor wouldn't tolerate any wrong moves, so I stayed bent over for a few more long seconds while she examined me with her cold eyes. Finally, she took the plate, and I straightened up, wincing at the pain in my lower back.

The bats put their empty vials on the floor, and the professor told me, "Leave us now."

I picked up the vials, put them on a tray, and guided the trays toward the door. The smell coming from the bottles was a disgusting mix of seaweed and rotten eggs.

"Yasmina," the professor said. "Open the window so we can enjoy a cool breeze."

The window glass slid into a wall behind the professor, and the sudden wind that blew in snatched away the sash that had been draped over my shoulders. The woman picked it up. She ran her hands over the sash, and asked, "A Pictipote silk sash and dress? But these are the clothes of a master. Why not put her in the usual slave's outfit?"

CHAPTER 8

My heart was pounding. The word *slave* was like a slap. Her eyes narrowed with hostility. Had I committed some crime without knowing it? I glanced over at the professor for help, and he replied, "My dear lady, you know that the clothes that the indentured usually wear are made from plastic fabric, and that I don't keep any plastic in my house. I have an old allergy to plastic, as you very well know!"

"And what about the sash?"

The professor gave a terse laugh. "The sash is easy to yank if you want to discipline her, don't you think? One good pull, and the clothes will tear right off her back."

The laughter of the bats sounded more like hissing. They surrounded me, and one of them put a paw onto my sash, so that it tore.

"A clever idea, Adam," the Golden lady said. "But I'd like to see how it works in real life."

She walked up to me and ran a finger along the sleeve of my dress, all the way up to my shoulder. She was toying with me, and it made her eyes sparkle with delight. The professor walked up to my other side, and I froze in place. Would he do as she said? And what if he did? I wouldn't be able to escape, not with these bats around! He reached a hand toward my shoulder, and I flinched. Then he took the woman's hand off me and said, "It is not my habit to discipline someone who has not erred."

Then he tugged at my sleeve and said, "Go away now. Yasmina, open the door for her."

I stumbled toward the door that had just opened and came out on the other side, panting. I leaned against the wall, catching my breath as tears slid out of my eyes. I had never felt more humiliated. This was how the indentured were treated. Their dignity dissolved by the bats' saliva.

And what was the difference between being indentured and being a slave? They were just different names for one fact—the fact of this collar. I tried to yank it off my neck for the thousandth time, but this time, I didn't try for long. My arms quickly gave up and fell to my sides. The ceiling seemed to be pressing down on me, suffocating me, so I went out into the garden.

Torn away by the bat's claws, my shoulder sash hung loose at my side. The bats' smell filled my nose, and I felt a disgust that verged on horror. Something about the events of the evening had completely unnerved me. I felt like I wouldn't dare snap my collar and run away. If they caught me, those deformed bat lips would turn me to ash in a second. It would be like a passionate kiss from a scouring pad. I had to find another plan.

I started crying again. I'd never been that close to a bat, and I didn't want to repeat the experience. Never again. The sash slipped all the way off my shoulder, and I nearly tripped over it. I pulled the two halves of it tightly. I'd have Dima bring me my clothes from the Burrow, and, from

CHAPTER 8

now on, I'd wear those. I walked away quickly, so that the bats wouldn't see me on their way out through the garden.

And that disgusting Golden woman—she'd enjoyed mocking me. She had made me bow to her for a long time, and she'd wanted the professor to punish me. I stood there so humbly—why hadn't I said anything?

I reached the far corner of the house, turned around, and headed toward the back of the building. If the professor hadn't sent me away so quickly, God only knows what else might have happened. Before today, I'd hated the professor a million megatons. Now, I only hated him a thousand megatons. I sat down on the ground, leaned my back against the house, and gripped my knees tightly, trying to calm down. I missed our apartment in the Burrow so much!

Suddenly, I heard a voice: "My sister the First Lady and her husband Zaher, who is the president of this island, want you to try again. You now know what's required."

It was the voice of that disgusting woman, and it was coming from a nearby window—the office window! This woman was the sister of the president's wife? That meant she was the Director of Security, General al-Azimi! Yes! The Director of Security was the first lady's sister! What did President Zaher want from the professor, and why had he sent his sister-in-law?

General al-Azimi went on: "I know this is the tenth attempt, but—"

"Eleventh," the professor interrupted.

"Adam, you don't need to remind me how many times my sister has tried and failed to get pregnant. Her sadness makes my heart ache. And yet, my heart tells me that this time, they'll succeed. Before we proceed, they would like you to amend your list of desired qualities. Of course, genes for leadership, cruelty, boldness, and so on. All of these should remain. But now, they would like you to raise the fetus's intelligence to 2000 or more."

Is that how things worked, then? Did they modify the genes of future embryos to ensure their superiority? It wasn't a coincidence, or fate, as they claimed?

"I'm at your service," the professor said. "However, I will warn you that intelligence this high usually comes with certain mutations, and we can't guarantee which direction the mutations will take."

She laughed. "Adam, I know you'll find a solution. This fetus will become the next president of the Comoros, and intelligence is a very basic requirement."

"I'll do my best," the professor said. "They still know the procedure, correct?"

"Yes, they know it well and followed it carefully. They sent you a refrigerated carton, and inside is everything you need."

I heard the professor accept the carton and bid his guests farewell. Suddenly, an idea struck me. Had I made a terrible

CHAPTER 8

mistake? This information was obviously highly confidential. Could they find out that I'd been eavesdropping on them? Could the bats hear my heartbeat through the wall? Should I sneak away? Or stay right where I was? I knew bats could sense movement, so I decided to stay where I was until they'd left. I tried holding my breath, but I couldn't do it for very long. After a few minutes that seemed like an entire lifetime, I heard the sound of the office door opening and closing. Then, a few seconds later, I heard the professor say, "Yasmina, open the external gate." Then he added, "Why didn't you tell me that the bats had arrived with a woman?"

Yasmina replied: "At 5:29, you said, 'Inform me when the bats have arrived.' You made no mention of a woman."

"You're stupid," the professor said.

Poor Yasmina. Everyone accused her of being stupid. This time she didn't say, *There's no need for insults,* the way she always did with me. Instead, she said, "I apologize, Sir. Next time, I will be more precise."

Even AIs respected the Goldens more than us! I was afraid the woman and the bats would fly over the house and see me hunched under the office window. I scurried under a clove shrub and watched them soar across the sky, ghostly silhouettes with the full moon behind them. The woman flew with her shoes, while the bats flew with their wings. They had been in a hurry to punish me before I'd even done anything. So what if I stole money and ran for freedom? I couldn't risk it—I didn't want to give these stinking bats the chance to come anywhere near me. I'd have to regain my freedom legally. I'd have to pay the professor those two thousand binars.

I could borrow them. But nobody had that much money! What about a competition? What if I won the award at the Quartzia Academic Excellence competition? I'd take Baba and Dima, and we'd run away from this terrible island to a place where no one was forbidden from wearing a Pictipote silk dress with a sash around the shoulders.

Was it possible that the indentured were allowed to participate in the competitions?

9

After General Al-Azimi and her bats had left, the professor summoned me back in. He studied me for a long time before he asked, "Would you like to go on a night cruise?"

As usual, my tongue jumped out in front of me: "Are you serious?"

And as usual, the professor didn't like it. He responded firmly, "I am always serious. Wash off your tears, put on clothes that aren't ripped, and let's go. A disheveled appearance seems to have become a treasured habit of yours."

I remembered the ashes from the fireplace a few days ago. "Yes," I blurted, "but stealing is more my speed."

I wished I could swallow my tongue! It was going to keep me from going on the cruise. I watched the professor purse his lips, as he always did. "The punishment for your wagging tongue is a new puzzle that you'll find waiting for you in the library tomorrow. As for now, prepare to go to sea."

The punishment didn't bother me, and the cruise instantly lifted my mood. I happily washed my face and got dressed in a flash. Before I knew it, I was waiting at the gate for the professor. I found Raji standing there as well. "Are you coming with us on the cruise?" he asked.

I nodded.

I hadn't known that he would be on the cruise, too, and of course I didn't call him, *Sir*. If Raji asked me to do that, I would break his oud over his head and let whatever happened, happen. I noticed that he was wearing turbo shoes, and I felt shocked at the sudden realization that it would be too far to walk to the sea. Would they send me alone on the lightning walkway?

I felt a rush of air brush against my side, and I turned to see the professor, who had just arrived wearing his turbo shoes, and was holding another pair in his hand. "Put these on and let's go."

Diyala in turbo shoes! What an impossible dream! When I took the shoes and checked the size, I said, "They're a bit big for me. They might slip off my feet."

The professor set his mouth in a straight line. "Fine. You can stay here if you want."

Before they could fly away without me, I slipped on the shoes. "Ready!"

Raji knelt in front of me to tighten the laces, and I squatted down, so we were at the same level. I was so embarrassed. I didn't know there were Goldens who were so kind and gentle.

CHAPTER 9

"Let me do it," I said.

"I just want to make sure the shoes don't come off, God forbid," he said. "You'd fall."

He was worried about *me*? I moved one of the shoes toward him. My heart, too. Tie someone's turbo shoes and get their heart for free! He tightened the first one, then stared at me for a few seconds, as though he were waiting for something. What did he want?

"How am I going to tie the other one if you're sitting on it?"

Quickly, I shifted my position. Then, once he was finished, I asked, "How do I make the shoes work?"

"First, you lean forward." He moved around to press against the hollow between my shoulders, gently pushing me forward. I followed his lead. "Now press your toes down against the sole of the shoe."

I had barely done it when the shoe shot me up and over the gate, where I started fanning my arms up and down in terror. Raji flew over and said, "Calm down, or you'll fall. Now squat. Squat!"

I got into a crouch, and my shoe stopped me, mid-air. The professor caught up and jostled around us. Raji grasped my hand. "The professor's patience is a bit thin. Listen, you just need to do what I do. Don't be scared. I won't leave you."

Then he straightened up and leaned forward, and I did the same.

"With only the tips of your toes, press down, light as a feather."

I did what he said, and we rose together. Then he grabbed my elbow tightly and steadied me.

"If you want to go to the right, then shift the ball of your foot to the right. But just a little. And if you want to go to the left, then shift it to the left."

Thoughtlessly, the ball of my foot twitched to the right, and the shoes took me to the right, away from him. But before I could panic, he caught up and took my arm.

"If you want to slow down, then press down with your heel."

This time, I didn't let my heel act on its own, the way it usually went with me. Instead, I took charge of my body. And after that, things got easier.

Raji smiled and whispered, "It's your first flight. Enjoy it."

Then I remembered that I was in the air! I looked around at the quartz houses in every possible color dancing and shimmering below us. I used to think that I'd only see Quartzia's dancing houses in the land of dreams.

CHAPTER 9

The quartz that the buildings were made from stored the sun's energy during the day, and then it used that same energy to light them up at night, as though they were shooting stars. And the magnetic waves that every living thing emitted were absorbed by the houses' quartz structures, which vibrated, making the buildings "dance." It was an incredible sight. Plus, the volcanic craters that dotted the island's surface were filled with blue water, and the jellyfish inside them made them glow a brilliant, phosphorescent green.

"Look out for minarets and tall water fountains," the professor suddenly told me. "Water ruins the shoes. And if you knock into one of the mosques' minarets, the shoes might break."

I had thought he was afraid for me, but, as it turns out, he was just worried about the shoes. Since the moment I set foot in his house six years ago, he hadn't said a single nice thing about me. I always felt that he held something against me. Although in truth, I wasn't a particularly big fan of his either, so maybe our feelings of resentment were mutual.

But at the same time, I never really felt that he *hated* me. It was something else, some mysterious feeling I didn't understand. When we got to the beach, Raji reminded me of how to land. Then he took my hand, and we descended together. My landing was so perfect, I felt like a seasoned flyer. The professor's boat was there, waiting for us. It looked like an oval dish made of thin, transparent crystal.

"What if it breaks under our weight?" I asked. "I can't swim!"

The professor ignored me, frowning as he quickly moved away from us, and Raji gestured with his arms that he'd save me if that happened, which made me smile. I smiled because I had discovered that I wasn't the only one who was afraid of the professor—Raji was, too. We silently boarded the boat, and it began to gently float us out onto the water.

"Let's hear you play, Raji," the professor said. "You'll find an oud I brought for you under the air pump there."

Soon, melodies poured from the belly of the oud. I hadn't known that stringed instruments could sound like this! At least I'd read about them, in a music history book in the library.

What would my life be like without reading? The only music that we ever heard down in the Burrow was electronic music. There were a few moments of silence, and then Raji started to play a tune I knew, the melody of the song, "Let Me Live Free." My mother used to sing that song to me.

"I know this one," I said.

"I know," Raji said. "I heard you hum it on the day we checked your vitals. I liked the song, so I learned to play it. It's a beautiful tune."

He learned the song in just a few days? That must be how easy things were when your brain was over 1111.

CHAPTER 9

I hummed along with him. Had he learned it for me? Or because it was a beautiful melody? He was an amazing musician. I remembered a story that was in a book I'd once snatched from the professor. In it, rats followed a man who played a flute all the way to the sea, because his music was so charming.

Here was a musician, and here was a sea, and I would follow this man wherever he went. I looked up at the sky, which was black as far as the eye could see, sprinkled with God's infinity of shiny dust. The darkness of the sea blended with the darkness of the sky, but I could tell where the horizon was, because the sea was a stretch of black in which there were no stars. Then there was the moon . . . I hadn't known that the moon could be this captivating! No wonder they named the Comoros after *qamr,* the Arabic word for moon. It could not be more beautiful anywhere else in the world.

As a girl, I'd only seen the moon in pictures. During the night, we were forced to stay underground, deep in the Burrow. We were buried deep in its layers of dirt, and its dampness seeped into our bones.

"Stunning, isn't it," Raji said.

How had he known what was on my mind? My mouth must have fallen open in astonishment, as usual. When would I grow out of this? Had I looked like an idiot, gaping at the moon?

"It's the first time I've ever really looked at the moon."

"I know," he said. "My family spent their whole lives in the Burrow, and none of them ever saw the moon. I'm the only lucky Golden in my family. Twenty-five years ago, the AIGL engineered me for free."

Wow. Every mother down in the Burrow dreamed that the Association for Improving the Genes of the Limiteds would engineer an embryo for her. But the association required that the family already have five children, and that the family's breadwinner be sick. Now I understood the secret behind his kindness. It was because his family were Limiteds.

His smile was sweet, and he had dimpled cheeks that made him look like those children from long ago whose mothers had nursed them with milk from their own breasts.

I pulled my shirt up to hide the collar I hated with every fiber of my being. I wished he wasn't a Golden, and I wished I wasn't indentured. Or that neither of us were citizens of Quartzia. Anyhow, I was leaving this place. Maybe . . . he would come with me?

"Do you think the Quartzia competitions allow indentured people to participate?"

"I haven't read anything in its bylaws that would suggest otherwise," he said, his eyes sparkling.

That was exactly what I'd wanted to hear. There was no law that stopped me from joining—but would I dare to do it?

CHAPTER 9

Just then, the professor's voice came to us from the helm, asking for orange juice. I hurried to make it without delay, since I hoped he would always bring me to sea with him. With Raji too, of course. I squeezed three spherical oranges of the same purple hue into a cup, and then I took it to the professor. He was lying face down on the boat's quartz floor, wearing a strange pair of glasses.

I got down on my knees and placed the cup beside him, hoping he wouldn't accidentally knock it over with an arm, since then I'd have to clean the floor of the boat. The professor lifted his head and took the cup. "Do you want to see the sea creatures?"

I looked down at the boat's crystal bottom, but I couldn't see anything beneath it except blackness. The professor took off his glasses and handed them to me: "Put these on and lie down, the way I'm doing."

I did as he said and lay down next to him. When I looked down through the crystal bottom, what I saw was the strangest sight of my life! Reddish creatures of all sizes and shapes swam in the water. These glasses let me see in the dark! I remembered the bats and shuddered—bats could see in the dark, too. I shook it off.

"I see a sawfish!" I said. "And a little shark. And a swarm of wild jellyfish, and a dolfish!"

I felt ashamed that I'd hogged the glasses for so long, and the professor was missing out, so I handed them back, saying, "A hundred years ago, there weren't any dolfish, but two separate creatures: a dolphin and a shark."

The professor gave me a look that felt deeper than the water beneath us. "Did you read that in one of my books?" he asked.

I flushed. "*The Animal Encyclopedia: Part V,* was about fish."

He put the glasses back on and sat there, watching the fish. I understood that he didn't want anything else from me, so I went back to Raji, who was still playing.

"All this beauty shouldn't be kept away from the people in the Burrow," I said. "All this beauty shouldn't be just for the smart people and government officials who're allowed to engineer their children however they want."

Raji stopped playing and stared at me in surprise.

"Diyaaaaaala!" I heard the professor behind me saying sharply. "Where did you hear this?"

Why had he invited me out here? He wanted to watch the sea floor, far below. And now, I had brought trouble. When would I learn?

"I heard the bats asking you to—"

He hurried over and covered my mouth with a hand, saying, "You will bring disaster down on our heads. Shut up, shut up. Swallow these words and forget them. Were

CHAPTER 9

you spying on me and my guests? If anyone heard this secret, all three of us would die. Do you understand?"

He shook my head so hard I felt my teeth rattle. He stood there, as if waiting for my answer. But how could I answer when his hand was covering my mouth? I nodded.

"From now on, you'll enter the library at five o'clock, and you won't leave it except to sleep. I don't want you to see any of my guests, and I don't want them to see you. Do you understand your punishment?"

Of course I understood. The language of punishment was more familiar to me than any other tongue.

10

With her long, graceful fingertips, Dima was planting tomato seedlings in the greenhouse soil. Today, when she'd showed up at the professor's house, every hair on her head had been a different color. As usual, half her salary had gone to the Eighth Floor Salon. The greedy woman who owned it fooled all the girls on our floor into thinking that they would walk out of her salon looking exactly like Golden girls. Imitating Golden fashions gave them the illusion that they were actually strong, empowered, privileged, and happy!

I told Dima about my adventure with the turbo shoes and the boat trip, and she said, "I'm *so* jealous. I'd give ten years of my life to wear turbo shoes, ride in a quartz boat, and hear music from a real oud. Plus watch the fish!"

"And I'd give ten years of my life for one night in the Burrow. I want to ride on the lightning walkway, go down the nanoparticle elevator, and sleep safely in our own apartment."

If I'd told her what had happened between me and General al-Azimi and her bats, then Dima wouldn't have wanted any part of my life. I was jamming a wooden stick down into the dirt, and she pulled it out of my hand and

CHAPTER 10

tossed it away. Then she sat down next to me and put her muddy hand on my shoulder. "Why did you go back to wearing your old Burrow clothes? You're not feeling well today?"

Her eyes insisted on an answer, so I gave her one: "Wearing the clothes that the Goldens wear won't make them respect us. I don't like their clothes, and I don't like them. We're just their puppets."

Just then, Baba walked into the greenhouse, catching the tail end of our conversation. The basket in his hand reminded me that it was five o'clock, and that he was here to pick fresh fruit for the professor, the way he did every day. Baba clearly knew I was hiding something, because he sat down next to us in the dirt and asked, with his hand gestures, "What happened?"

My chest was still tight from everything that had happened yesterday, so I blurted out: "The bats came to visit the professor yesterday, and they humiliated me."

I remembered the word *slave*. The stench of the bats had bored its way into my memory, and I could hear the sound of my sash being torn, again and again. Baba pointed to his tongue and motioned anxiously, asking, "Did you fight back?"

"I wish," I said sharply. "I wish I'd faced up to them, even if I'd died. Better than the life of a slave that I have here. I don't even know what's happening to me. Every time we're insulted, I just stand still and do nothing."

Baba's hands chopped through the air, as though he wanted to scold me. But then his expression softened, and he grabbed me in one quick motion and pulled me against his heart. I knew that he couldn't bear to lose me. He kissed his hand, the way he always did when he wanted me to remember Mama. Then he pointed to his tongue and my tongue. He was reminding me that my mother had a loose tongue, and that I looked a lot like her. Then he squeezed me tight and put his palm against my mouth. Baba's strong embrace was demanding that I swallow my words and be silent. The Goldens wanted me to shut up. He wanted me to shut up. Even *I* wanted me to shut up.

Then the professor's voice emerged from my wrist: "Diyala, go quietly to the library and don't leave there before eight."

I stood up angrily and told Baba, "Ok, fine, I'll shut up." Then I headed for the house. Three hours of imprisonment and puzzles awaited me, so that the professor and his guests could enjoy their meetings far from the ears of slaves. For the next thirty months.

Dima followed me, saying, "I can't stand it anymore, either. Walking past the elevator bats every day without you by my side is terrifying. Every second, I feel like they're going to drop down and kidnap me. The Burrow without you is a grave!"

I knew that being away from me made Dima feel orphaned all over again. I struggled to control my anger as

CHAPTER 10

I tucked a strand of hair behind her ear and said, "It's going to be ok. I promise."

My plan to win the prize *had* to succeed, so that we could be together again. But I couldn't tell her about it, because I couldn't guarantee that she'd keep it secret.

She pushed my hand away and spat, "The last time you said that we were on the lightning walkway. And then, an hour later, they put that collar on you."

She turned on her heel and strode away. I knew that her words were supposed to sting, but I wasn't angry with Dima. Soon, I was going to win the finals, be freed, and then we'd be back together under the same roof—in the Burrow, or anywhere else in the world. Soon, everything was going to be ok. I walked into the library and closed the door behind me. I thanked God that the second round of the academic excellence competition was set for today.

"Yasmina," I said. "Show me the competitions channel. And let me know if the professor is coming near the library."

"I can't do that," she said.

This time, I didn't insult her. I felt sorry for her. As I started working, it occurred to me to ask her, "Yasmina, do you always tell the professor where I am and where I'm headed?"

"Only when he asks me," she said.

"And when did he ask you today?"

"He asked me at 9:33, 10:25, 11:18, and—"

"You're a snitch," I said.

"There is no need for insults."

Every time I tried to be nice to Yasmina, she was mean to me. But she was the only one around for me to be friends with.

"Do you take photos of me, too?" I asked.

"Photography is forbidden in Professor Adam's home."

I knew that, but I just wanted to make sure. Unlike all the other Goldens, the professor didn't have his house monitored by cameras. I was relieved that she'd confirmed it.

"Yasmina," I said. "Show me the Quartzia Competition the minute it starts."

She agreed, and I wasn't sure if I'd even finished a couple of shelves when the studio appeared in the center of the library. The match had begun.

Sikmadar appeared, as usual, with a huge smile that showed off his two front teeth, which glittered with a star made of diamonds and a sun made of some kind of red stone—I didn't know what it was called. Just like last time, the virtual concierge welcomed me, saying, "No. 2114442, welcome to the brilliant academic excellence competition. Your seat is number nine. Up on the contestants' platform, of course."

CHAPTER 10

Einstein appeared, along with the laser control armor, so I put it on and walked Einstein through the theater, until I reached the contestants' platform and sat him down. I saw the contestant who'd called himself Dinosaur of the Sea last week, sitting nearby. I didn't remember the rest of the contestants, since I'd been too busy serving a meal to the professor, which meant I'd missed most of the show.

With his fakey Golden accent, Sikmadar said, "A great deal of excitement awaits us in today's matches. Right now, we have ten contestants. But by the day's end, there'll be just five. The five weakest contestants will head home, and the five best will stay. We're looking for the five who have mastered the world's universal language—the language that lifted our small island to the ranks of the great powers. And that, ladies and gentlemen, is the language of mathematics."

Mathematics was a subject that schools down in the Burrow barely taught. They gave us just enough so we could calculate how many balls of massage ointment would be enough for four Golden toes, if one ball was enough for two toes. The introductory music started, and I found myself inching to the edge of my seat, my whole body turning into a pair of ears.

"The first question of the day is: Use the number eight eight times to get to the number 1000. Only addition is allowed."

I closed my eyes and imagined eight numbers spreading out in front of me in different formations. The secret, of course, was in the one's place. How do we add the number 8 so that it gives us 0 in the one's place? Suddenly, the solution appeared in front of me, and I slammed down my hand. Einstein's hand hit the answer button in front of him, and a whistle sounded, which meant the rest of the contestants were prevented from answering.

Sikmadar walked up to Einstein and said, "Will Einstein be able to give us the first correct answer, just as he did in the last round? Well, let's hear it."

I said: "888 + 88 + 8 + 8 + 8," and Einstein's lips moved just like mine did, with the answer.

A wide smile broke out across Sikmadar's face. "Congratulations to you and to all of us here in Quartzia for this academic excellence. Our first finalist is Einstein. A seasoned and dangerous competitor. Einstein, my friend, tell us something about yourself so we can get to know you a little. For instance, give us one of your pearls of wisdom."

I was stunned and remained silent for several seconds.

Sikmadar tapped Einstein on the shoulder and laughed. "Our friend here is a little shy." He went on: "Shyness is a rare quality here in Quartzia. But in any event, we insist on hearing from you, Sir."

"My wisdom is this," I said, slowly. "Don't let anyone else put limits on you. You're the only one who decides how high you can go."

Everyone was silent, and it looked like Sikmadar was a little confused. What was wrong? But then his expression

CHAPTER 10

relaxed, and he said, "All right, my friend. And now, we're going to ask you to leave this seat and go be the first to sit on the finalists' podium."

I got up and walked over, and Einstein imitated my movements until I got him up onto the podium and sat him down. The spotlight swept back and forth over Einstein several times, and his image appeared on the big screen. Underneath his image, there were comments from the viewers at home: "Well done, Einstein." "Clever!" "We're proud of you." "Are you a student at the Quartzia College of Advanced Mathematics?" "What's the secret behind your strange name?"

I smiled. Finally, one of us Limiteds had succeeded in catching the Goldens' attention! I wondered what they would've written if they knew I was a Limited. It would inevitably be something like "cheater" or "stupid," or something like that. The lights went out, and darkness blanketed the studio. Questions followed questions, and it hadn't even been an hour when I found four other contestants sitting next to Einstein—and the Dinosaur of the Sea was one of them. The lineup for the finals was now complete, and Einstein was one of the final five. I leaned over and whispered to the dino, "Congratulations to the both of us, my friend. Praise be to God."

As Einstein whispered those last few words, I laughed, which made Einstein laugh. The closing music started to play, and images of the candidates appeared on the screen. The dino appeared, followed by shots of him taken from today's episode. There were scenes from last week's episode, too: a shot of the dinosaur applauding himself, and another of him muttering, and more. The other three contestants were shown, too, but Einstein didn't appear anywhere in the montage.

I waited. Then the screen went totally blank, and it stayed that way for several seconds. What was going on? Was it because of my whispered comment? Had they kicked Einstein out of the running? Or had someone found out about me?

Finally, a clip of Einstein appeared—the one where he'd given the correct answer at the start of the episode. After that, they showed him up on the finalists' podium, muttering the second answer to himself before the others responded, then a shot of him muttering the third answer, and the others. I didn't know that the camera had been on Einstein the whole time! I'd actually known all the answers right away today, and I guess I'd muttered them, and Einstein's mouth had imitated my movements. Now all the viewers knew what I'd done.

There was silence for a few seconds, and then the whole studio erupted in applause. The other competitors turned and looked at Einstein with expressions of dismay, having seen what he could do, except for one avatar that had turned his hair into the branches of a cherry tree. This one smiled at Einstein and patted him on the shoulder.

As for Dinosaur of the Sea, he stood up and jabbed a finger into Einstein's chest, saying, "Don't be too pleased with yourself. It's the final result that counts."

CHAPTER 10

Then Sikmadar walked up and held his microphone out to Einstein, asking, "Do you think you're going to win the whole thing?"

I fell into a stunned silence. Win? I moved back, as though the microphone really was in my face. That meant Einstein stepped back, too, which made everyone laugh.

"This contestant sure is quiet," Sikmadar said. "But doesn't his shyness just add to his mysterious charm?"

The audience cheered, the curtain fell, the studio disappeared, and the library fell silent.

What would General Al-Azimi have said if she'd known that Diyala Karthala was one of the five contestants vying to win the Quartzia Award for Academic Achievement, even though she was categorized as a "slave"?

11

"**Dinner will be served at a later hour one night this week,**" Professor Adam told me, Baba, and Dima. "On Thursday evening."

He had summoned us to his office in a hurry, and now he glanced in my direction. "The invitees are powerful people, including senior economic officials here in the Comoros. I want everything in the drawing room to shine like gold."

I hated gold.

He continued, turning toward Baba. "Nabil, I would like to serve traditional foods. Ask Yasmina about the menu, and Dima will provide you with fruits and vegetables from our farm."

I felt a surge of pleasure, because this meant he'd need to send me to the old market to go shopping. I hadn't left the house in ten days, except to go on the cruise.

"How many people are coming?" I asked.

The professor must not have liked that I'd interrupted him, because he ignored me, continuing to speak directly to Baba. "A store called Baqala has been sending me its advertisements, claiming that its products aren't genetically

CHAPTER 11

modified. Have Yasmina order everything you need from that store, and the delivery balloons will bring it. Let me know if there are any complications. Leave now."

My hopes of going to the market evaporated. We headed for the door, but before I could step out, the professor said, "Ten."

When I turned and gave him a questioning look, he said, "Ten people are coming to the dinner."

So ten influential people would be coming on Thursday. I hoped ten misfortunes would fall on their heads. Griffin bats would probably be coming, too. The trace of my recent experience with people in high-up places still showed on my sash. I had lost some of my dignity that night, and I would never get it back. Now, I pulled out the cleaning cart and headed for the guest room.

There, I found Raji practicing the oud. He had set a music book in front of him that was made out of cellulose paper. It looked like the books in the professor's library. The song he was singing was called "High Above the Palm Trees," and it was one of my favorites. It had been sung a hundred years ago by a singer called Sabah Fakhri.

I leaned against the cart, listening to the words of the song, "It's hard for me to be away. I miss them, miss them." Tears filled my throat as this sad melody reminded me of my own sad reality. I missed them, too. But who? Or what? I didn't know.

Suddenly, Raji noticed me and stopped playing. As he usually did when he saw me, he stood up and welcomed me. "You look down," he said.

"I'm fine."

He gestured for me to sit next to him. "I'm going to play at the dinner, but I'm really nervous. The people he's invited are as VIP as you can get."

When I looked into Raji's golden eyes, they were filled with worry. I'd never seen golden eyes look worried before.

"But your playing is amazing," I said. "You're going to blow them all away. You just have to practice every day until dinner so that none of them will find anything to nitpick."

"I can't," he said. "The professor needs me in the lab. He's working on a very important invention—a nourishing fluid that will keep human organs alive for years. I barely have time to practice two hours a day. But don't worry about me." As he said these last words, he gave me a tender smile, and his boyish dimple appeared. If only I had golden eyes, too . . . But no, it would be impossible for me to ever get them. The penalty for getting a transplant of golden lenses was death, and the penalty for buying or selling golden contact lenses was five years in prison. The difference in eye color would separate us forever.

"Diyala," Yasmina said. "I would like to remind you that, based on your effort exerted in previous days, the amount of work remaining for you today will require you to spend

CHAPTER 11

an additional 43 minutes after five o'clock, and you are not allowed to—"

"Yasmina, shut up."

"Does the professor still send you to the library every day at five?" Raji asked. "What do you do in there?"

Does he still send you? That was a nice way of putting it, even if it didn't describe what was actually going on. What he should really say was, *Does he still lock you up?*

"I dance," I said. "Or I talk to myself. Sometimes I read, and—and I whispered this last part into his ear, so that Yasmina wouldn't hear me, "if I don't finish the book, I smuggle it into my room and stay up reading it."

He whispered back, "Would you like the professor's permission to take the books with you to your room, so you don't have to smuggle them out?"

His breath smelled of mint, and I whispered back, "He'd never let me. If he thought it was ok for me to borrow his books, I wouldn't be here in the first place."

A strange feeling came over me. It was as if Raji and I were actually one person, even though I'd never touched him, and he'd never touched me. I wished we could stay on that couch forever, but Yasmina was right. I didn't want to spend the night solving puzzles, and then fail and get punished again.

I stood up. "I'll leave you to your practicing and get back to work. I don't want to disturb you."

"I'll finish up practicing and come help you."

But before I got back to work, I saw Dima waving at me through the window. I gestured to Raji that I wanted to go outside. But I didn't say anything, so that Yasmina wouldn't rat me out. I pointed to him, to my mouth, and then toward the door. He seemed to think for a few seconds, and then he grinned and said, "Yasmina, open the door for me."

"Yes, Mr. Raji," Yasmina said. Then she opened the door, and I quickly slipped out into the garden. Dima pulled me into the orchard, in among the vanilla trees, where she handed me a small leaden box. "This box is from Daddy Three Arms. There's a really powerful magnet inside, so you have to make sure you're in a room without any iron in it before you open the box. Open it for ten seconds, then close it, and all the programming will be erased from the collar."

I glanced behind me, an old reflex of mine, then took the box and slipped it in my pocket before anyone else could see it. Yesterday, Dima had been so angry when she'd left that there hadn't been a chance to tell her I was too scared to run away. After what had happened, I was terrified of what the bats might do to me. Plus, now I had a backup plan, even if I couldn't give her the details. But before I could slip the box back to her, so that she could cancel her arrangement with Daddy Three Arms, she said, "Daddy Three Arms says you should keep the collar on so that you won't attract any attention. You'll meet him in the elevator

CHAPTER 11

courtyard on the day he sends you a satmail. You'll have to check your metacrystal tablet several times a day. And he wants a thousand binars from—"

"A thousand binars?" I cut in. "What a thief. I don't need this plan anymore, so you can give him the box back. There's another, safer way to do this, and it'll leave me with plenty of money. I just need two weeks."

Dima insisted that I tell her about this other plan, but I refused. She swore to me a thousand times that she wouldn't tell a soul, so finally I gave in and told her about the competitions: about Einstein, Sikmadar, the Dinosaur of the Sea, and everything. When I finished, I didn't find the relieved expression I'd expected. Instead, she said, "You're so stupid. Do you think they're actually going to let you *win*? When will you understand that we Limiteds never get to win anything? And that nothing good ever happens to us?"

She started to breathe faster and faster, as if she'd run a thousand miles. Then she burst into tears. What was going on with her? I couldn't bear to see Dima in pain like this, and I knew it wasn't just my story upsetting her. I grabbed her wrist and squeezed tightly. "Tell me the truth. What's bothering you?"

"I entered my name in the Dreamland lottery."

Her words crashed onto my head like a titanium column. Then I pushed her away from me. "Are you crazy? Dreamland means I'll never see you again for the rest of my life. Baba will never see you again. Have you totally lost your mind?"

She walked up and shoved me in the chest. "Do you think that after Daddy Three Arms smuggles you off the island, we'll ever see *you* again?"

"I was going to bring you both over the minute I arrived in the nearest country, idiot. Did you really think I was going to abandon you?"

I grabbed her head in both hands and asked, "Don't the rumors about Dreamland scare you? God only knows where the government is taking people. Nobody ever comes back."

She wrenched herself away, backing up into the trunk of a vanilla tree and sliding to the ground. "Why would anyone ever want to leave Dreamland and come back to the hell of the Burrow? Even if the government kills the people it takes to Dreamland, I don't care. Death is better than the so-called life we're living. Nothing changes here except when it gets worse. Look what happened to you."

I knelt down next to her. "The lottery drawing will take place right after the last round of the competition. That's in just a few days! What if you win the lottery? You just, what, disappear?" I smacked her across the face and asked, "Do you even realize what you've done? Now we have to run away fast, before the lottery drawing. All of us—you, me, and Baba." I wanted to slap her a thousand times, but the professor's voice rang out in my ears. He sounded as though he was about to explode. What now?

12

I still wasn't sure about leaving the cover of the vanilla trees when I found the professor standing there, waiting for me. His face was as white as a ghost's, and his eyes flashed. He grabbed my hair so tightly that his nails were practically digging into my scalp. He twisted one of my arms behind my back so hard he almost broke it. Then, my head bent down, he pushed me in front of him.

Dima tried to pull me out of his grasp, saying, "Please, Professor. Please leave her. She didn't do anything." But he was so much stronger than I had ever realized.

Still, Dima planted herself in our path, not budging.

"Your sister's actions are going to land us all in prison," he said. "I'm going to teach her a lesson. Get out of the way or I'll punish the both of you."

Dima stayed right where she was, as firm as a statue. He must think I'd passed on what I'd heard from General al-Azimi. But I hadn't told anyone! I was afraid of what he might do to Dima, so I told her, "Dima, don't worry about me, I can sort this out."

She stayed right where she was, not moving, so I shouted, "It's a misunderstanding! I just need to explain things to him. Get out of the way now." She hesitated another few seconds, then stepped out of the way.

He shoved me along, as though he were pushing a goat, until we reached the house. Then he yanked up my head, brought my ear close to his mouth, and muttered angrily, as though smoke were coming out from between his teeth, "How dare you join the Quartzia competitions, you crazy girl! And, on top of that, say those crazy things?"

How did he know about the competition? Had Yasmina told him? But I'd only said eight numbers in front of her, so how could she know? Impossible! So who had told him? I knew this man wasn't going to show me any mercy. What would he do now? Would he kill me? Would he hand me over to the Griffin bats?

Raji was standing on the steps that led up to the house. Raji was well built and capable—he could save me. I called out, "Raji! Please, help me!" But he didn't move. He just stood there, watching, while the professor dragged me into the house and pushed me toward the kitchen.

"Don't just stand there like that!" the professor shouted at Raji. "Go get me some rope from the fishing locker."

Raji hurried off to do his bidding. Even Raji? Goldens were all the same. The professor yanked open the kitchen door and the two of us went in, followed by Raji. I wished Baba were here. But what could he do? One sick man against two Goldens who were both at least twice as powerful as him. I was paralyzed, my arm twisted behind my back. I tried to

CHAPTER 12

trip the professor, but Raji reached down and grabbed hold of my feet. Was this how he helped the professor?

"Why, Raji?"

He wouldn't look me in the eye.

The professor flung open the basement door and pulled me down the stairs. We were near a bottle rack, but there was nothing on the shelves that I could grab and throw at him. The professor pushed me forward, and I slid, sandwiched between him and the wall. The professor pinned my arms while Raji tied my ankles with several knots. I tried to kick at his hand, but the professor gripped my neck so tightly, I stopped. He brought his face up close to mine and said, "Do you know the name of the crime you committed? Identity fraud. Identity fraud means—"

"I know what identity fraud is, you miserable old man!"

"And do you know the penalty for identity fraud? Raji. Go to my office and fetch what I told you to get."

That thin bamboo rod . . . Raji was definitely going to bring the bamboo rod. My heart collapsed, falling down between my trembling knees. A piece of it broke off, sliding to the floor. This time, the professor would definitely whip me. That was why they'd tied me up, I was sure of it. He'd been waiting for an opportunity like this for a while. Why had I put myself in this position?

"Please," I said.

He grabbed my shoulders and shook me. "You have brought me nothing but misfortune. Nothing but misfortune! But I have the treatment for it."

I bit down on my lip and started crying. His grip on my shoulders was so strong that the pain was almost unbearable. Then, a few seconds later, I heard Raji come back down the stairs. His steps, as he walked down the stairs, almost made me faint. But when he finally appeared, he didn't have a bamboo rod in his hand. No, it was books!

He set the books on the floor in front of me as the professor said, "You're going to stay locked up here until you've read all of these books, and I'm going to test you on the first one tomorrow."

Then he let go of my neck, and the two of them headed toward the door.

"Yasmina," the professor said. "Do not speak to Diyala and don't answer her, either. Do not open the door for anyone but me. Do you understand?"

"Yes, Sir," Yasmina said.

Then he ordered her to open the door for them, and she obeyed him. They disappeared through the door, and then it was closed up again.

Once they were gone, I massaged my shoulders, wrists, and arms. That old man had nearly broken my neck and my hand, and he'd almost ripped out all my hair. He was

CHAPTER 12

so cruel! I stood up and yanked at the rope with all the anger bubbling inside me. If there had been bottles on those miserable shelves, I would have broken every single one of them.

The rope got tangled up, and I stumbled and fell to my knees. What was going to happen now? Every time a door opened in front of me, my bad luck slammed it shut. First, the professor found out I was borrowing books, and then he made me into a slave. Then, when the big prize was finally so close, the professor found out I was in the contest. How had he found out? It must've been Raji who snitched. I'd asked him in the boat whether non-Goldens were allowed to join in the competitions. He must have guessed what I was doing from that and ratted me out. Dammit! Why had I underestimated him? All the Goldens were so *clever*.

And on top of all that, Dima had entered her name in that shadowy lottery. I leaned against the wall and imagined Dima down in the Burrow. I hugged the air as if I were hugging her, and I started to sob. Why did Mama have to die and leave me as a surrogate mother for Dima? A mother at seven? I gulped in a breath, and memories swept through me against my will. I remembered giving her my energy drinks instead of drinking them, and how we would sleep together on my narrow platform. How we imagined that Baba's toes were little bombs we could throw at the bats.

How could Dima do this to me? How could she throw herself into the scary unknown? My head was heavy with dark thoughts—I couldn't run away with Daddy Three

Arms because I was too afraid of the bats, and I couldn't be in the competition because of the professor, and the worst thing of all was that Dima might win the lottery. Finally, my brain's engines ran out of whatever juice it was running on. I ran out of breath. Darkness surrounded me, and despair finished me off. I lay my tired head on my knees and fell into a deep, deep sleep.

13

When I opened my eyes, I had no idea how long I'd slept. It was dark down there, and I didn't know how much time had passed. When I asked Yasmina what time it was, she didn't answer. Obviously she remembered that the professor had told her not to talk to me. Scattered snapshots from the nightmare I'd had still clung to my eyelashes. The strange thing was that I hadn't dreamed about Dima, or the professor, or about the bats. Instead, my dream had been about the frightening stone bridge down in the Burrow. I had been endlessly running and running and running, while my mother's voice called out behind me, "Diyala, run, get away!"

Beside me, I found a box of foul-tasting energy cakes, a large bottle of water, a box of balloons to pee into, and a halogen butterfly for light. Someone must have brought these things down here while I was sleeping. I was very thirsty, but the water bottle was so big, I couldn't tip it up to drink out of it. I looked around for something to pour it into, but I couldn't find anything. I tried to untie the rope around my ankles, but there were a lot of knots, maybe six or seven, and they made a tight nest of tangles. I unwound the rope as much as I could and searched every spot I could reach, but all I found was one forgotten bottle on a rack in the empty closet. I picked up the disgusting thing. It was empty except for a small amount of blood. I dumped it out on the floor, then tipped the big water bottle so I could rinse it out several times before I drank from it.

I was sure it was Raji who had brought all these things while I was sleeping. The co-conspirator. I dipped my finger in the blood I'd spilled out on the floor and wrote a message on the wall: GOLDENS AND EVIL SHARE THE SAME MOTHER.

Then I pulled out an energy bar and bit down on the foul thing. This was the kind of food that kept people in the Burrow alive and working. It was cheap and tasted bad, but it kept you on your feet and at your job. The only advantage was that it dissolved completely, leaving no waste, so that you no longer had to go to the bathroom.

Now, I felt energy flowing through my bloodstream, and it reached my exhausted brain and perked me up. I had to find a backup plan, since the competition was no longer an option. I'd have to escape Quartzia before the lottery and the finals. And Baba would have to escape with us, so the government wouldn't take revenge on him. Daddy Three Arms would get us out. I'd have to flee during the hours I was locked in the library; that way, the professor wouldn't notice I was gone. And if he didn't report me, then the bats wouldn't know I had fled. All I had to do was get out of this gloomy basement and find a stash of money in the house for Daddy Three Arms. But, if I wanted to get out of the basement, then I had to read all these books. Or at least that's what the professor had said.

CHAPTER 13

I held them up close, examining them, and I discovered that there were three books and a music capsule. The butterfly lamp lit up, and I read the first book's title: *The Art of Drawing and Its Schools Throughout History.* Then there were two collections of poetry, one by Nizar al-Qabbani and another by Ghassan Kanafani. I'd never had an interest in learning about music, drawing, or poetry, so how was the professor going to test me in these subjects? And why was he doing it at all?

Was he just trying to keep me busy so I wouldn't do something even more foolish? But if that were the case, he could've just sent me back to the Burrow. So . . . no. He wanted to punish me. That was why he didn't choose math or physics books. Instead, he'd picked the kinds of things I wouldn't be interested in. He must want me to stay down in this gloomy hole forever. But no, he wasn't going to be rid of me that easily! I would give in and memorize these books, because I didn't want to spend the rest of my life tied up down here, in an empty storage room inside a dark basement.

I decided to start with the art book, which I thought must be the easiest. I paged through and found a lot of names, like Rembrandt, Asaad Arabi, and Leonardo da Vinci. I knew that last name, at least. They had a picture of his most famous painting, the Mona Lisa, in the book—it was an empty-headed woman with a naïve smile. I read about the painting. It had been in the Louvre before that museum was destroyed by arial bombardment during WWIII. That's when the painting had disappeared, along with the museum's other treasures. The book explained the secrets of this painting and many others. It explained about the impressionist, abstract, and classical schools of painting, ending with the Laser School, which had been popularized nineteen years ago. I didn't feel the time passing, but I was hungry again. I read some more, and then I got hungry. I read and slept and read and drank and read and filled seven balloons with pee.

Finally, after a thousand years, the door opened, and the professor came in. This time, he was alone. Where was his loyal dog Raji?

He bit his lips, the way he always did when he was about to do something really bad to me. When he came in, I hadn't stood up out of respect, the way I was supposed to, and I intended to maintain this good habit. He sat down on a solid smoke chair and asked, "Have you read the books?" I handed him the one I had finished. Without opening it, he asked me, "Who painted 'The Starry Night'?"

"Van Gogh," I said.

"And 'Night Watch'?"

"Remblant."

He corrected me patiently, "Rembrandt."

Then he asked me several more questions, most of which I knew the answers to, before he took the book under his arm and nudged the sofa's smoke out of my range of movement with his foot. Then he left. He was afraid that

CHAPTER 13

I'd rest my bones on a couch instead of on this hard floor. What a creep.

So had I passed his exam? I thought so. A smile crept across my face. My plan to escape from this arrogant, cruel man was still on track. I closed my hand around the butterfly lamp, and its light went out. I slept.

When I woke up, I pulled out the music capsule. I pressed its button, and a laser sketched its contents in the air: Qudud Al-Halabiya, Andalusian Muwashahat, Fayrouz, Umm Kulthum, and lots of other things I'd never seen in my life. The first song was called, "Hand me the Flute and Sing," and it was beautiful.

The songs went on, and each one was more beautiful than the last. There was "When She Seemed to Sway" and "You're My Life" and a song called "Red Mars." It had been sung by a woman named Sawsan Makouk al-Qamr on the day the first group left Earth to live on Mars, back in 2044. I didn't find it hard to memorize what was on the capsule. No, it was easy to commit the lyrics of those nineteen songs to memory. But when the professor stepped inside, I flinched. I hadn't realized that another 24 hours had passed.

The exam was just like the exam the night before—or the day before. I wasn't sure which it was, because I had no sense of time in this dark basement. He sat on the solid-smoke couch, and I didn't stand, and our eyes didn't meet. This time, he didn't correct a single answer. And when he stood up, he took the music capsule with him.

I blurted out, "Can't you leave the capsule here?" As soon as the words were out, I regretted them. Of course he wouldn't. And he didn't disappoint—he held onto the capsule as he walked out the door. I hated him so much!

I tried to keep to the same routine with the book by Nizar al-Qabbani, but it didn't work. Lots of the poems were about love, and they irritated me. "Love has a scent, and it can't help but smell like a grove of peach trees." That's what the poet said. What lies! Maybe he'd been lucky in love, but I knew for a fact that not all love smelled like peaches. I looked down at my feet. Some loves smelled like feet tied up with a heavy rope in seven knots. Why had I trusted him? How had I thought he was different?

Hours passed, and I didn't make any progress with the book. Now I understood why the professor had chosen this particular punishment. He wanted me to die of boredom. I asked, "Yasmina, are you here?" but she didn't answer. I said, "Yasmina, you're a stupid, useless, bald idiot," but she didn't tell me that there was no need for insults. The silence was deafening, and the darkness was like a series of merciless blows to my eyes. I threw the book away, and it was swallowed up by the darkness.

Oh, God, what had I done? How was I going to find it now? I placed the butterfly lamp on the tip of my index finger and stretched out my arm in front of me, moving as much as my ankle rope would allow, but found nothing. After I despaired of finding it, I decided to read the only book I had left: Ghassan's book. I walked carefully back

CHAPTER 13

toward it, but on the way, I tripped over something and stubbed my toe hard enough that I cried out. I brought the light down toward it and saw a box. This box looked like the one in the office, and it had the letters "AA" on it. I turned the key that was perched in the lock and opened the lid. It was full of makeup, moisturizing cream, shiny stockings, and a paintbrush that reminded me of my mother.

Whenever I wanted to, my mom had let me draw on the walls of our apartment. Dad would tell me, "Don't waste the paints" and Mama would tell him, "It's ok, I'll bring more."

I was sure that I'd been with her when she died, but I couldn't remember any of it. I'd been only seven when it happened, and all I really remembered about that moment is that she told me, "Run away." Maybe she had been attacked by thieves, and she'd run from them? But she hadn't managed to escape?

A rock started to expand between my lungs, the way it always did when I tried to remember what had happened that day. I stood up and put the brush back in its place. I was about to close the lid when I saw it. There! In the corner, at the bottom of the box! It was a box about the size of a ball. I took it out and opened it, and inside I found what I needed most of all: jewelry! Rings, earrings, and necklaces made of platinum; man-made obsidian diamonds and hybrid oyster pearls. This stuff must be worth a fortune! I didn't even need a fortune—all I needed was three thousand binars for me, my dad, and my sister, and a little more to start a new life once we were off the island. The price of an ounce of platinum was three hundred binars, and each of these rings and earrings were at least an ounce. I pulled out a single handful of the jewelry and shoved it in my pocket. Then I closed the small box, followed by the larger one, and put it back in its place. Finally, un unexpected twist of fate that was good!

After that, I followed the rope back to my place. I'd barely gotten there when the door opened again. This time, it was Raji. I turned my face away from him. He sat down on the floor a little ways away from me and picked up Ghassan's book to ask me about it, but I told him I hadn't read a word. I asked him to find Nizar's book, which I had flung into the darkness, and he used the metacrystal disc on his wrist as a flashlight so he could find it for me. He asked me a few questions, but I didn't answer.

"Didn't you read anything between yesterday and today?" he asked.

"I read it," I said. "But it was all total nonsense about love."

"I know you don't want to see me," he said. "But the professor has an important appointment with General Azimi, so he sent me instead. Diyala, listen, I . . . I had to help the professor."

I threw the glass water bottle at him. He dodged out of the way, and it shattered.

CHAPTER 13

"My advice is that you read the last two books, because you won't get out of here until you do."

I pretended not to hear him, so he got up and left. But even though I was angry with him, I followed his advice. I was going to read these two books, get out of here, sell the jewelry, and escape from this island. I just had to find a way to drink, now that I'd broken my bottle.

14

The next day, or anyhow at a time I thought was the next day, the professor came down. He asked me questions about the two books, and I answered most of them. Then he flopped back against the solid-smoke couch, as if he had been the one taking the exam, and said, "I'm going to let you out of the basement today, on one condition—that you forget about the competitions. I'm going to go out there in the finals round, lose, and go home. No one will ever know that you impersonated me and did the first two rounds in my place. That's the only way we can both avoid the consequences of your reckless behavior. Is that understood?"

Who said I was going to sit around Quartzia, waiting for the competition? I had to get away as soon as possible, and the jewels in my pocket had opened a path for me. I nodded, but he said firmly, "I want to hear you say it."

"Of course I won't really go to the finals round. Do you think they'd let an indentured servant beat them out? I was just having a little fun."

He snapped his fingers in exasperation. Sometimes, I felt as though he were about to hit me. "Well, I hope you had

CHAPTER 14

sufficient *fun*," he said, glancing around, as if gloating over my sentence down in the basement.

I ignored him, and he went on, "Tonight, you'll leave the basement, since I have a dinner party. My guests, as I've told you, are very important people. Thus, they do not like being served by eight-armed robots. You and Raji will take care of them."

Robot octopuses had hyper-advanced programming that helped them sense guests' needs and meet them immediately. Why would his guests reject a thing like that?

"Unlike an octopus, I don't have e-cigarettes in 189 different flavors, and my arms don't have induction heating magnets so that the food reaches you while it's still hot."

This time, he didn't bite his lip, the way he usually did when I provoked him. Instead, he said, "You seem to like staying down here in the basement." Then he got up.

"I'm sorry . . . Sir," I begged. "Please let me out of here."

"Even the *slightest* mistake today, and I'll lock you up down here for a month. You'll be by yourself, tied up with a rope just one meter long, after I've shaved your hair off so you look like a pumpkin!"

He never seemed to be joking. I felt my ears redden with anger.

"What if your guests are the ones harassing *me*? You saw what happened last time."

"You will not interact with the guests. Everything will be ready on the table. You'll stand just outside the door, and when Raji asks you for a juice, for instance, you will mix it up in the kitchen. I know you're good with juice blends. So is that clear?"

I had to go along with him so that he didn't punish me again and delay my plan. Subconsciously, my hand felt for the rings in my pocket as I said, "Clear, Sir."

The professor looked at me with suspicion, probably because of my sudden subservience, so I added, "Do you have any slave clothes that would fit me?"

I caught a glimpse of a smile twitching at the sides of his lips. He quickly wiped it away and said, "Shower and put on any tidy clothes. Do not wear a sash. Today, the laser projector in your room will show you a videogram about the geography of our islands and their surroundings. You will watch the entire series. Finish it today, and tomorrow I'll test you on what you've learned. And I want you ready at seven p.m. in the dining room. Is that clear?"

I agreed, and he cut the rope with the laser scissors he'd brought with him. He walked toward the basement door, and I followed. As soon as I stepped out, I found Baba and Dima waiting for me. I hugged Baba, but then I felt bad, because I knew I smelled awful, so I cupped his cheeks in my palms and moved his head away.

I looked over at Dima, and she looked at me. Our last meeting hadn't been ideal. But when I opened my arms to

CHAPTER 14

her, she threw herself into them. How could this silly girl have ever thought we could live without each other?

Next, I hurried to my room. I had barely stepped inside when the laser projector lit up, and a map of the Comoros Islands appeared. Were all professors this obsessed? I continued my forced viewing of the episode as I filled the quartz tub with warm water. I took off my clothes, pulled the rings out of my pocket, and shoved them in the pocket of my down jacket, which I'd put away in the silicone wardrobe.

Then I slipped into the water and was greeted by the sound of electric pumps massaging every muscle in my body. This spa treatment almost made me forget the hateful parts of living in Quartzia. After the bath, I lay down on the solid-smoke mattress, but I couldn't sleep because the laser projector was continuing my lesson. As I watched, I realized that, down in the Burrow schools, they hadn't taught us geography.

I started to watch the videogram with avid interest. After all, I had to know everything about the countries around us, since I didn't know where Daddy Three Arms would dump us. Then it was afternoon, and I opened up the silicone capsule. I wanted clothes that were neither luxurious like silk, nor artificial like the Limiteds' clothes. I found a black dress with a label that said, "Treated fabric, maintains constant 82 degrees, absorbs moisture, glows purple in the dark." I put it back in the capsule. Tonight, I didn't want to light up. I wanted to disappear. I found a long navy-blue linen shirt with white pants beneath that didn't quite reach my ankles, and I decided this was what I wanted. Then I combed out my hair and tied it up with a clasp. The letters AA on the comb reminded me of the box down in the basement with the rings, and I whispered, "Thank you, AA."

When I emerged from my room, Raji was tuning the strings of his oud in the main hall. I ignored him and went into the kitchen. Baba was changing his clothes and Dima was carrying a large platter toward the dining room. I ran up and helped her carry it. "You look amazing," she said.

I set the platter down on the round table's warm surface, and I told Yasmina, "Set the tabletop's temperature to 88."

"Done," Yasmina replied.

The center of the table rotated, and whenever a plate passed in front of one of the ten guests, they could serve themselves from it. They would be fine, even without the octopuses.

Dima whispered to me as she straightened the utensils, "Do you remember Tamer al-Sharif? The waiter at Café-19, who was one of the Dreamland lottery winners last year? Yesterday, I met his sister in the secondhand-clothing store, and she told me . . ." Dima's voice fell away as her eyes filled with tears. She took a breath and went on, "She told me that, in these last couple of weeks, she's started to suspect that the video messages her brother's been sending from Dreamland are fake, because she recognized a scratch

CHAPTER 14

on his neck—it was a scratch their little lion hybrid gave him three years ago. It was right beneath his left ear, and it should've been completely healed. The government is using old images of the winners to make the current videos. Tamer's gone. And I'm afraid that if I win the lottery, I'll be gone, too. The Quartzia competition's in two days, and the drawing comes right at the end!"

I wished I could just leave her hanging, so that she'd suffer a little for her stupid decision, but my heart wouldn't let me. "I have an escape plan for all of us," I whispered. "Don't worry about anything. I've got the money. Just tell Daddy Three Arms that he has to arrange an escape tomorrow for all three of us. Everything's going to be ok."

She nodded, and then she threw herself into my arms. This time, she believed me when I said that everything would be ok. But I still had to find a way to believe it myself. She and Baba were in a hurry to leave the professor's house, since the elevators would shut down in just half an hour.

Shortly after they left, the guests arrived. This time, not a single bat entered the house. Although there *were* Griffin bats, they all stayed outside. This was a comfort to me as I muttered to myself that the evening would go well.

The dining room door was left open, and I stood in the hallway beside it, waiting for Raji's instructions. I spotted General al-Azimi, although this time without her bats. That cursed woman stood up and said, "First, I'd like to thank the professor for hosting us today. And then I'd like to tell you all the real reason for this celebratory dinner. Our great leader President Zaher and his wife are expecting a beautiful child. And today's dinner is to break the news."

Everyone clapped and cheered. Was there anything more beautiful than a president who could guarantee them an extension of all his privileges for another fifty years? Then one of the guests said, "Let's turn off our metacrystal tablets. That way, we can be at our ease, and we won't have to worry that any of these nosy devices will record what we're saying."

"Of course," everyone agreed.

I suddenly realized why the serving octopuses hadn't come out of their closet today. The politicians were afraid that their words would be recorded. Raji stepped up and handed me a large bowl of tablets. "Hi," he said shyly. "The professor says to put it out on the hallway table, so that the guests can take theirs on their way out."

I took the bowl from his hand without meeting his gaze and set it out on the table.

After that, there was a lot of clanking of spoons on plates and murmurs of admiration for how well-cooked this dish was and the mix of spices in that one. Then one of the guests said, "So. That competitor Einstein, the one who everyone's talking about. What do you think about what he said, 'Don't let anyone else put limits on you . . .'?

Einstein? My ears were wide open now.

CHAPTER 14

One of the guests answered quietly, "The man surely wants to cause riots in our peaceful country. May God give him no help!"

A female voice disagreed: "I don't think he wants to cause a riot. The girl who polishes my teeth told me that everyone down in the Burrow will give him their votes. He said it to get their votes, that's all. There's nothing else to it."

The professor interrupted. "I would like to make you all special juices from my well-loved traditional trees. Each of you, please, tell me your favorite blend of flavors."

He wanted to steer the talk away from Einstein. Now I knew why the professor had gotten so angry that he'd thrown me down in the basement. It was because of that single sentence I'd spoken with Einstein's mouth. And I'd done it from his device, at his home address. The organizers would think that the professor was Einstein, and that this was an insult coming from him. Why had I said such a stupid thing? Raji was standing near me, at the dining room door. Now, he walked up and whispered, "I swear, I didn't breathe a word about the competitions to the professor. General al-Azimi was the one who told him. She sent him a sat-mail that said, "Congratulations, Mr. 2114442, for qualifying for the third stage of the Quartzia competitions for academic achievement. I thought you hated mathematics, Adam dear!"

I guessed Raji was probably telling the truth, but I didn't say anything. I heard General al-Azimi respond to the professor's offer, asking, "Do you have mango with yellow watermelon?"

"I have mango and strawberries," he said.

Raji stepped away from me and quickly recorded her request with an electric pen, so that her words would be saved on his tablet, which he'd placed in the basket with the rest of the tablets so that no one could secretly record their fellow guests. After that, the rest of the requests poured in, and Raji hurried to record them all. When they were finished, he went into the hallway where I was standing, took his tablet from the basket, and handed it to me.

"All the guests' requests for juices are here. I hope you can read my handwriting."

His voice was low and filled with shame. I took the tablet with the tips of my fingers, with all the meanness that fingers could convey, and went to the kitchen. The first line was, "The Director of Security's drink, General al-Azimi, mangoes and strawberries." I mixed together mangoes and strawberries, then glued the word, "General" to the base of her cup. The second line read, "Mr. First Judge, peach syrup, no sweetener." I poured out juice from the peach bottle in his cup without adding red-seaweed sweetener, then wrote "Judge" on his cup. After that came the Minister of Metacrystal Communications, who wanted coconut and pineapple with ice, and then a drink for the

CHAPTER 14

owner of the Energy Bar Company. Next, I made the drink for the owner of the Barq pedestrian walkway, followed by all the rest. I got it done in under ten minutes, placed the cups on a flying tray, and turned the tray's light spectrum a shade of violet.

It looked so elegant like that—iced and shining with dew, bursting with brilliant flavors and colors. All it lacked was . . . a little delicious spit from my mouth! I spat in the first cup and looked at it. My saliva foamed up beautifully on the surface of the juice. I repeated it in the second and third cup when, suddenly, I felt breaths on my shoulder. I turned and found Raji looking at me in confusion. I shot him back a challenging look. What would he do now? Would he chain me to the ultraviolet sterilizer? He moved closer to the tray, looked down at the juice for a few seconds, and then . . . spat! He spat again before he smiled at me, saying, "I never knew that saliva was an essential ingredient in smoothies."

Against my will, I smiled back. "That's because, before this, you didn't know me."

Side by side, we worked on finishing our joint spitting mission, until we came to the cup with the professor's name on it. Then we hesitated. Raji said in a low voice, "Einstein's comment really was dangerous. It was better for you to be in the basement than for both you and the professor to fall into the hands of the Griffin bat guards. That's why I helped him. Believe me." He nodded at the cup. "I think the professor prefers his without spittle."

"As you wish," I said. Now that I understood Einstein's comment was the real reason behind my imprisonment, I no longer wanted to spit in the professor's cup.

Raji peeled the labels off the cups. "I memorized them, so no need for these." Then, together, we guided the giant tray down the hallway.

"I'm sorry!" he whispered, and his eyes seemed sincere. Everything around us disappeared, so that only he and I remained, with just the cups between us. The cups had a scent, and they couldn't help but smell of peaches.

We reached the door. The moment we entered, I heard General al-Azimi ask the old man sitting beside her, "And how did you find Tamer al-Sharif's heart and pancreas?"

Tamer al-Sharif was the waiter who Dima had told me about—the one who'd disappeared! The old man laughed. "That waiter! His pancreas is working well, and his heart is amazing. All thanks to you for having the idea for Dreamland."

Dreamland was an *organ bank*? My hands started to shake and let go of the tray, so that it hung in the air. Then it had a collision, tilting wildly so that several cups crashed to the ground before Raji could catch them.

Insults rained down on me from everyone around: "Clumsy girl!" "Slaves are so useless." "How stupid!"

Raji laughed and said, "My fault, my fault. The metal rings on my apron caught on the edge of the tray." Then he turned to me and said in a stern voice," Go get the mop

CHAPTER 14

and bucket. We don't want cleaning snails tonight." But I was still so shocked by what I'd heard that I couldn't move. Raji smacked me on the shoulder and said, "Are you deaf?"

Then he gave my arm a warning squeeze, so I hurried to bring what he'd ask for. As I ran out of the room, I heard him ask the guests, "Who would like to listen to that old song, 'You're My Life'?"

When I reached the utility closet, I pulled out the bucket and mop with shaking hands. Dreamland was actually an organ bank! How stupid could I be—why hadn't I realized it before? After all, wasn't everyone who won the Dreamland lottery young? Why did these people need to have everything—people's money and their livers? And Dima, that silly idiot, had gone to them on her own two feet and put in her name. We had to get away from these criminals as soon as possible. Daddy Three Arms would have to get us out of here tomorrow.

15

When my duties were finished and the guests had left, I went to my room and threw myself down on my bed, feeling like someone who'd just swum to Australia and back. What I'd heard today at the dinner party had wounded me to the core; these Goldens were storing us up in a giant jar called the Burrow as potential spare parts for their worn-out bodies. I tried to sleep, but I couldn't. A cold hung around me that drove deep into my bones.

I hugged my pillow and yanked a faux bearskin blanket up to my nose. There were a hundred times more of us than there were of Goldens, so how had we allowed this to happen? How could we accept any of this? We did their jobs in exchange for money they gave us with one hand and took away with the other, selling us make-up, disgusting energy bars, and satellite network subscriptions. A volcano of anger boiled inside me. Had Dima gone to Daddy Three Arms and told him that the money was ready, to speed up our escape? I whispered to the tablet in a low voice, so that Yasmina wouldn't hear me, "Do I have any new emails?"

"You have received an email from an account called 'Cloves' that says '555.'"

CHAPTER 15

Dima had explained that Cloves was the name Daddy Three Arms would be using, and that I had to add two to each number to get the date of our escape. So if 555 + 222 was 777, that meant the seventh day of the week, the seventh hour, and the seventh minute. The seventh day was tomorrow!

Tomorrow was going to be a long day, so I had to sleep right away. I tried and tried to fall asleep, but I couldn't find a way in. I climbed out of bed and went to get a sleeping pill from the kitchen's mini-pharmacy. Every time I opened up that medicine cabinet, I was surprised by the range of injections that were available. For sleep, for diarrhea, for itching, for coughs. I didn't know exactly how to use it, so I decided to watch an online tutorial. On my way back to my room, I heard the piano in the sitting room. Was Raji still here? I walked up to the room and heard General al-Azimi speaking to the professor. The door was closed, so I couldn't tell what they were saying. Was she scolding him for what Einstein had said? I burned with curiosity.

The dressing capsule in the guest room had a cylinder that was half in the guestroom and half in the dining room. I hurried to the dining room, stepped into the capsule, and closed the door behind me. Then I pressed my ear to the door that opened onto the sitting room and squinted. When my eyes adjusted, I could see them through the sliver of space around the door.

General al-Azimi had just finished playing a song, and the professor was leaning against the piano beside her. He applauded stiffly and said, "Well done, Madame al-Azimi."

"I miss the days when you called me Lina. Ah, those were the days."

The professor pulled back his hand and remained silent.

"Ever since you met that redhead, you've turned away from me and never come ba—"

"I left you long before that," he cut in. "We parted ways when you decided to join Security. Don't you remember the day? I begged you not to. They had just released the Griffin bats, and everyone knew that the government of Quartzia was going to use them to terrorize the Limiteds. And now you've become their right-hand man."

"To terrorize or to establish security? This is dangerous talk, Professor, and you wouldn't want anyone but me to hear it. And it's strange to hear such things coming from you. After all, you're the one who improves the genes of the children of the powerful in Quartzia to ensure they remain in power. Doesn't that make you their left arm? Maybe we're more alike than you think, Adam."

"I want the best for everyone, rich and poor, Golden and Limited. Have you forgotten that I'm the one who established the Association for the Improvement of Limited Genes?"

I hadn't known the professor was the one who started up this association, or that he worked for it, although I

CHAPTER 15

knew it had its jellyfish-like headquarters on the corner of Griffin Street. The lines of people standing at the door in order to get their name on the list stretched all the way to the Street of Infinities. Everyone dreamed of having a child with golden eyes to support their family.

"I take care of one fetus, free of charge, for every family with a sick breadwinner who has five children. And if the Quartzian government allowed it, I'd improve everyone's genetics. You know that."

The government prevented him from improving everyone's genes! Why was I not surprised? After all, their privileges were based on our shortcomings.

"Adam," General al-Azimi said. "The reason I've stayed behind is to warn you about what you said in the latest round of the competition. As you heard, everyone is talking about it—even your guests. I'm confident that you didn't mean anything when you made your avatar throw out that bombshell, 'Don't let anyone else put limits on you.' But how else were we supposed to understand it?"

I squinted at the professor's expression. The muscles of his face had tightened, and General al-Azimi went on, "To the Limiteds, such sayings might suggest that they need to reject the limitations that we have placed upon them. And then what would happen to our island? And to us? The president was furious at your little comment, but fortunately, the contents of the cooler you sent us helped your case. It has worked amazingly well, and now my sister's blood, after all these years, is full of pregnancy hormones.

We thank you for your service, Adam, and of course for the dinner."

She stood up to leave, ending her speech by saying, "The finals are in two days. So choose your words carefully, my friend."

The professor turned and headed toward the closet. Before I could flee my hiding place, he opened the door. I almost fainted from terror. It felt like a ball of thorns had gathered in my throat. The professors arm patted around in the coats, then pulled out a fur coat and closed the door. I turned and hurried out of the closet, through the dining room, and ran barefoot to my room, where I dove under the covers. I injected the sleeping drug into my arm without watching any video about how to do it—I just tried to remember what we'd learned in school. Within seconds, it started to take effect. If the professor had seen me in the darkness, and came here to demand an explanation, he would find me asleep.

<>

The next morning, Dima and Baba didn't show up for work like they usually did. When I asked Raji about them, he said, "The professor gave them the day off. They've been working really hard the past few days, and they were exhausted from the harvest and from preparing the food." Raji was in the garden, collecting the empty bottles of blood that he'd distributed to the bats the day before, along with their delicious insects.

CHAPTER 15

Why weren't Dima and Baba here today? I needed to spend the day with Baba to convince him that my escape plan was solid, even though I didn't think he'd hesitate once he heard what I'd learned last night about the organ bank. Would Dima be able to convince him?

Raji must have noticed my confusion, because he said, "Don't worry, I'll help, and together we'll get everything back in order."

Yeah, sure. I wished that tidying up the house was the only thing I was worried about.

I took out all the cleaning snails and released them around the house. Then I gathered up all the plates and cups on a trolley, pushed them into the dishwashing room, and selected the "boil" cycle. Anything that had been touched by the mouths of these disgusting people would have to be sterilized.

Then I poured out some of yesterday's leftover juice and took a cup out to Raji. His head was practically melting in the sun as he drove around the mechanized rinsing elephants, with their long hoses, to remove the bloodstains from the grass.

When he took the juice from me, he asked, "Did you spit in it?"

"Oh!" I said. "I forgot!"

He drained it all in one gulp and then said, "You know what? I wouldn't have . . . I wouldn't mind. I mean, I wouldn't mind if you did. If your spit was . . . ."

A drum pounded inside my chest. Was he declaring his love for me? I didn't think this day could get any more complicated.

"Raji," I said. "Yesterday, I was watching a videogram about Ajuran, and I thought about how much I'd like to live there. There, nobody oppresses anyone else. If my dream comes true, what do you think? Would you like to go, too?"

"I'm ready to go with you to Mars," he said. "Life without you . . ." But he didn't finish his sentence. If only he knew, at that moment, how close he was to living without me! I would send for him, when we got wherever we were going, and he could follow us.

The disc on my wrist buzzed, and the professor's voice emerged: "Diyala. I want you in my lab with dinner at seven this evening. Don't interrupt me before that."

At seven o'clock, I would be with Dima and my father in the elevator courtyard, on our way to freedom. The thought made me smile.

"The professor's putting the finishing touches on that nourishing serum I told you about," Raji said. "He told me not to interrupt him either, so I'm going to take the chance to be gone for the day. I'm giving a concert on Mwale Island. The host's submarine is picking me up soon. But I'll be back the day after tomorrow, God willing."

I smiled at him. "Bye." Then I followed him with my gaze. God only knew when I'd see him again.

CHAPTER 15

The minutes passed slowly until finally it was six thirty. I put on my simplest clothes—a white cotton dress with a high neck that hid my collar, and a lot of bulky fabric that didn't show the shape of my body. It was long, almost down to my ankles. Underneath, I put on tight white leggings, so I'd be covered in case our escape included crawling, swimming, or something like that. In this dress, I wouldn't attract any attention. All I had to do now was disable the collar.

I tried to think about which room would have the fewest metallic items, and I couldn't come up with anything better than the library. So I took the small box that Dima had given me and went there. In a spot that had nothing but bookshelves and a velvet sofa, I opened the box. I didn't feel anything, but a globe with an iron base rolled off a high shelf and flew toward the box sitting in front of me on the table. I caught it at the last moment, right before it made any noise. I hadn't seen it, but God had protected me.

I decided the magnet inside the box must have worked, deactivating the collar's software. So I closed the box and quickly returned to my room, pulling the rings out of the down jacket and putting them in my pocket. Then I went to the window, so that Yasmina wouldn't notice me opening or closing a door, and I chose a place that couldn't be seen from the laboratory window. Then I slipped out.

I ran as fast as I could until I got to the old market. Then I walked carefully along its edge. What if the magnet hadn't really deactivated the collar? Slowly, I took my final steps. Would I be struck by a bolt of lightning that would paralyze me, like I'd seen happen to that child? But I passed the old market, and nothing happened. The magnet had done its job.

A giant sunflower arrived, and I stopped, glancing around at the people around me. It had been just two weeks since the last time I was last on the walkway, but it felt like two years. The sounds of ordinary passersby spooked me, as though someone was following me. I tried not to glance around too much, so people wouldn't get suspicious.

When I saw the giant elevator platform, I started to relax a little. I stretched my gaze to the far side, where the elevators were, and I felt a longing rise up inside me. Who would've thought that I would miss the Burrow? And that I loved it and cared about its people? The shadow of the cypress in the square seemed to have grown heavier. As usual, bats were hovering above everyone's head. I headed for the elevators, where I was supposed to meet Baba and Dima, but I didn't find them there.

The crowd was thick, so I thought maybe they were waiting and I just couldn't see them. When I widened my eyes, I saw Daddy Three Arms standing in the shadows near the electricity-capsule vendor, watching me. He gave me a warning wink, and I pretended not to know him. I looked around again, searching for Baba and Dima. Did he know something about them? I decided to get a little closer to him.

CHAPTER 15

When there were only a few steps between us, I saw a shadow racing toward me so fast that my heart jumped out of my chest! Without thinking, I started running as hard as I could, but a silent gust of foul-smelling air hit me and then . . . my feet were in the air!

16

In her flying shoes, General al-Azimi raced on ahead of the bat that had snatched me up, its talons gripping the back of my dress. All at once, the darkness of the Burrow descended and surrounded me, and I saw myself as a seven-year-old girl, walking with my mother along the stone bridge. I saw a bat hovering above us, and I told Mama, "It's so ugly." She clapped a hand over my mouth, but it was too late. He'd heard me. He pounced on us, snatched us both by the hand, and lifted us into the air. When my eyes fell on the lines of his face, I screamed. Mama smacked him, and he growled, letting go of me, so that I fell a few meters and hit the ground.

"Diyala, run!" my mother said, over and over, but I didn't. I just stood and watched as the bat flew with her until it reached the black void at the center of the Burrow and then . . . threw her in. I rushed to the edge and watched her disappear into the darkness. The screen inside my brain showed her falling a hundred times clearer than it had actually been, and it repeated the exaggerated sound of her clothes flapping, again and again.

I opened my eyes and came back to reality. The bat held me with its talons, and the horrible general flew on ahead of us. Terror paralyzed me. I was afraid that, if I moved, I

CHAPTER 16

would fall and break my neck. I wished I had my mother's courage to smack him, so that he'd let me go, and I could join her. But while I'd inherited her spirit of confrontation, she had not passed on her courage.

I closed my eyes, trying to shut out what was happening. Would they fly me to Sarwa? They said People who entered Sarwa never left again. Would they sell me off for parts? Would the bat put its carbon sponge lips on me, suck all the liquid out of me, and transform me into ash in seconds?

I felt the bat's claws release me, and my eyes flew open in terror. We were a meter or two up in the air. I fell, hit the ground, and rolled several times. The rings fell out of my pocket and scattered in different directions. When I got up, I saw that I was in the professor's garden. General al-Azimi landed in the grass, as did the bat, which brandished its whip.

At just that moment, the professor appeared in his doorway and ran toward us. The bat and General al-Azimi were behind me. I was surrounded.

"I was leaving my office in Sarwa when I caught sight of her. I knew immediately that she'd run away. She stole from you, too."

The world was falling down on top of my head. My mother's voice rang in my ears: "Run, Diyala, run!" So I ran with all my might in one last, desperate attempt to escape what was waiting for me. But I could already hear the whiz of the whip's tail as it rose into the sky. I fell on my knees and wrapped my arms around my head, waiting for the tail to strike me. But instead, a weight fell on my back, blocking the sting. The professor! The blow struck him, hard, and I screamed, but he didn't! He just curled in on himself without falling over. The general ran toward him, reaching out to help him up, but he stood and raised his hand, waving her off as he said, "I'm fine."

"She stole from you and ran off," the general said. "She deserves to die by this whip. Why are you protecting her?"

With some difficulty, the professor straightened up. Then he said, "I sent her to the market to see how much the rings might sell for. They're old and engraved, and the expert on sat-net couldn't give me a proper estimate."

"She resisted arrest," Lina said. "She must be punished."

"She won't be able to withstand the whip," he said. "It will kill her at the first lash. You know that. I need her."

"Oh, do you care about this girl? Do you *love* her?"

The professor brayed out a small, brittle laugh. "Lina, have you lost your mind? Diyala is my chef's daughter. She's the same age as my grandchildren. I'm running tests on her."

The general turned around. "There's pride in her eyes that needs to be extinguished. Either you punish her, or I will."

The general set a palm on my trembling shoulder, but the professor tugged me away from her, saying, "I'll punish her."

CHAPTER 16

The professor didn't wait for her reaction. Instead, he just pushed me in front of him toward the house's front door. I hurried to obey. I no longer cared what he was about to do to me—this man had just saved my life.

Once the three of us were inside his office, he opened the drawer and took out the bamboo rod. He bent it several times, so that it was horseshoe-shaped, as though checking its flexibility. Then he waved it in the air, so that it gave off a chilling sound. A stone dropped from the top of my stomach to the bottom, and the general flashed her teeth.

I couldn't move. The professor pressed his hands on my shoulders, pushing me down so that I fell to my knees. Then he tore at the back of my dress. A chill licked my back with its rough tongue, and I shivered. I gripped the edge of the table that stood in the middle of the room, holding on so tightly that my fingertips had turned white. I promised myself I wouldn't let go. Then I took a deep breath, closed my eyes, and waited.

I will not scream, I will not scream, I repeated to myself. The professor tapped my back lightly with the stick several times, as if numbing my skin with it, and then he held it there for a few seconds. I took a deep breath, and then "sssssooowhhhshhhh." For the first few seconds, it didn't hurt. But then it was as if a thousand bees had stung my back.

"Awwwawwwaawwwwwwawwww!" A scream escaped my lips. The pain was growing every second. I shook my torso back and forth, hoping the throbbing pain would ease, but it didn't. Or rather, before it went away, I was struck again.

This time, the pain came right away, and it was worse than the first time. How many more stings would there be? I couldn't possibly hold on! General Al-Azimi walked around the table to get a look at my face. I clenched my jaw tightly to hold in my screams, but they overpowered me and escaped my mouth, getting louder with every blow. Without thinking, I started to crawl away, trying to escape, but the general grabbed my hair, shoved my face down, and set her shoe on my shoulder.

"I hope you, the bats, and all the Goldens in the world rot in HELL."

After that, lashes rained down on every part of my body, which failed me. Every lash tore a gasp or a scream from my chest.

"She's still proud," that woman said. "I want to hear her say, 'I am nothing.' Keep going!"

The blows kept raining down on me until I was moaning like a wounded mare. The professor shouted at me, "Say it! Say it!"

But I didn't. Instead, I screamed, "Enouuugggghhhhhhh! Owweeeenough!" And repeated those words until I fainted.

17

When I woke, I was still on the office floor. The professor knelt next to me, supporting himself on his elbows and taking deep breaths. The general had left. It took me several seconds to grasp just how much pain I was in. My back felt as dry and scratchy as a locust's wings, and every inch of my flesh screamed with pain.

"Diyala," the professor moaned. "I need . . . I need your help."

Sweat was pouring off him. His face was a milky white and his lips trembled. "That lashing from the bat's whip has gotten the better of me. I need two capsules for the pain. Get them from the medicine cabinet. And get one for yourself, too."

I tried to stand, but I couldn't. I pushed myself up using the edge of the table that had witnessed my suffering. Once I was up, I walked one-shoed, dragging my feet toward the kitchen. When I brought back the capsules, the professor told me to give him an injection under each armpit, so I did. After that, I injected myself.

"Ok," he said. "Now the next task. The whip secretes a burning poison. I need a mirror, ohhh, a mirror, and some reparative ointments. But they aren't in the medicine cabinet. They're down in that chest in the basement, the one where you found the rings. Can you do that?" He gasped with pain. "At the bottom of the chest, you'll find a blue liquid-nitrogen capsule. In a compartment inside, you'll find the three ointments."

The basement stairs were long. If I went all the way down them, I wouldn't be able to climb back up, not in my condition. "I can't," I said. "Let's call Raji."

"Raji's on the island of Mwale, far away. You're the only one who can help me."

Carefully, I tried to get him up on the couch. With every movement, he made a heart-wrenching moan. The bloody red wound was an inch-wide ribbon that ran from his right shoulder down to the left side of his waist. He repeated, "The bat's whip secretes—"

"I know all about the bat's whip," I interrupted. "It's a flagella hybrid, part organic."

"Then bring me a knife. And some sterilizer, too.'"

On my way to the basement, I passed a mirror in the lobby, where I peeked at my reflection. The white dress was torn and stained with blood. In the places where the fabric was torn, I saw rows of red lines, glowing and hot. I ran my fingers gently over my back and upper thighs, to see the extent of the pain. A thousand wolves gnawed at me. But then I pulled myself together and continued toward the basement. As quickly as I could, I did what the professor

CHAPTER 17

had asked. But when I stretched out my hand with the ointments, he couldn't take them from me.

"The paralysis is starting to take effect. You'll have to cut my shirt off with a knife." He buried his face in a sofa cushion and turned his back to me. I cut the fabric and tried to pull it gently away, but the blood and damaged tissue were stuck to it. He moaned, and I stopped. "Pour the sanitizer all over my clothes," he said. "Don't worry, it won't burn me."

I dumped disinfectant over his clothes until they were wet. Then I tried again. This time, the cloth came off easily, and I threw it away. Underneath, I saw a frightening sight: his shoulder bone and part of his spine were exposed, surrounded by a mess of nerves, muscles, tissue and skin.

One blow had caused all this? The Goldens' bones were twice as strong as ours, and so were their muscles. This blow would have split me in half.

"It looks pretty serious," I said, struggling to keep my voice steady. "You need a doctor."

"Treating a bat-whip wound is prohibited by law," he said. "I won't find any doctor to help me."

I rubbed at the bridge of my nose, trying to think, then asked him, "So what should I do?"

"First, sterilize your hands. Then mix the ointments, pour disinfectant over the wound, and apply them. The ointments will do the hard part."

I did what he'd told me. Although the disinfectant didn't burn him, the weight of it falling on his open wound made him scream. I ignored him, since his back needed a lot of sterilization. When I spread the ointment over his back, it felt so hot, it was almost burning. I tried to be gentle, but the groans that emerged from the pillow were deafening. How could he have possibly raised his hand to smack me with the bamboo rod, again and again, when his back was like this? Every blow must have torn his wound even more than it tore mine.

I felt sick with pity. I needed to go back to the medicine cabinet for bandages. When I was done, the professor was still, so I lay down on the carpet beside his couch and fell asleep.

When I opened my eyes, sunlight filled the office. The professor wasn't on the couch, so I got up and looked for him. I walked out of his office into the hallway and found him coming out of his bedroom. He was wearing only pants and a light flamingo-feather scarf over his shoulders and back.

"How are you now?" I asked.

"Better," he said. "The ointments you applied are very effective. Will you reapply them?"

We both went back into the office, where he took off his feathered scarf.

CHAPTER 17

"Wow," I said. "The difference between yesterday's wound and today's is huge. There's already a layer of thin, silvery skin covering the whole thing. It's a miracle!"

"Hardly. The ointments are made with stem cells from the umbilical cord of someone close to me."

That made me remember my pain, which had faded only a little. "You're lucky. I wish I had an ointment like that."

He answered with the firmness that I'd been used to: "No one ever died from being hit by a cane."

I sterilized his wound again and changed the bandage. Then I set the feathered scarf back over his shoulder. He handed me a small glass jar and said, "Put this ointment on your back several times a day. It will relieve the pain and prevent scarring."

I took it from him and headed for my room, dreaming of a warm tub and fresh clothes. But suddenly the kitchen door opened, and Baba stepped out. He must have just gotten here, and he'd heard our voices. When he saw my clothes, his eyes widened. His eyes sparked with fury as he looked at the professor, and then he attacked him like a missile, shoving him hard against the wall, so that the professor screamed out in pain. Baba pulled back his arm, ready to throw a punch, but I just managed to catch his fist.

"Baba, the professor saved my life."

With a wave of his hands, Baba asked me who'd done this to me, pointing at my back.

"The professor," I said. "But . . ."

After that, he didn't give me a chance to explain. Instead, he pointed to his pockets, then spread his fingers in front of my eyes, nodding at the professor.

"Baba will work for you for ten years, to pay off my debt to you."

"I understand Nabil's language," the professor said. "There's no need for you to translate."

Baba got closer to him, fixing the professor with an angry stare. Then he rubbed the edges of his index fingers together and pointed at the door to the house. He wanted to take me home with him. I'd never seen my father so angry as he was today.

The professor stared at him for a while without answering. Finally, he smiled and said, "We have a lot of leftovers. There's date and hazelnut pie, and plenty of juice. Let's all have breakfast together."

I answered quickly, to defuse the tension. "Absolutely, I'm dying of hunger. Baba, please, let's eat."

We had never sat down at the same table with the professor before, but we did on that day. Me and Baba. Then the professor called Dima from the conservatory, and even Raji showed up and sat with us.

CHAPTER 17

When Dima saw me, her eyes widened with shock. "What are you doing here?"

I ignored her question and whispered, "Why weren't you with Daddy Three Arms yesterday?"

"He said that that indentured servants were smuggled through a different route from the one used for Limiteds, and that yours was more dangerous. He told me that he'd smuggle you out yesterday first, and then Baba and I would go on Thursday. What happened?"

My father had put his shirt on over my dress, so Dima hadn't noticed my condition.

"Baba, Dima, and Raji," I said. "I have something to tell you." Then I relayed the whole story: how I'd planned to escape and smuggle out Baba and Dima, how I'd stolen the rings in order to pay the smuggler, how General al-Azimi had spotted me as she was leaving work, and then how the professor had defended me and had been badly wounded for his trouble. When I finished, Baba was wiping sweat from his upper lip, Dima was sobbing loudly, and the professor was looking gravely disappointed.

"I did it for Dima," I said. "She put her name in for the Dreamland lottery. So we had to get her away from here. We still do."

Baba grabbed Dima's wrist and gave it a questioning shake. She nodded in confirmation.

After that, Baba dropped his head into his hands, unsure what to do, and Dima burst into more tears.

The professor stood up. "Diyala and Raji, come with me into the lab."

18

I found myself lying, once again, in the cocoon-like coffin, the helmet and goggles on, cuffs on my ankles and wrists. Raji's hand was in mine, helping me forget the pain of the coffin's hard surface against my wounded back. The professor's eyes were fixed on the screens in front of him.

"What's happening?" I asked Raji.

The professor interrupted: "Hush."

I remembered that the professor had told the general he was doing experiments on me. What kind of experiments? When the ringing and buzzing finally stopped, the professor gave a wide smile, and his eyes were glazed with tears. He tried to turn away, but I'd already seen them.

"Miss Diyala Karthala, let me be the first to congratulate you," he said. "Your IQ has reached 1119, and you have officially become eligible to receive a pair of golden eyes."

My eyes widened in disbelief. I looked at Raji and found that his expression confirmed what the professor had said.

"But isn't the IQ machine at the National Center for Golden Irises?" I asked. "Why would it be here?"

"This machine is connected to the National Center for Golden Irises," Raji said. "The government provided it for the professor's laboratory because he needs it for his research."

The professor took my hand and sat me down in a chair opposite him. "When you calculated the area of a circle with a radius of 79 meters in just one second, I couldn't help but notice your mathematical prowess. It was even more impressive because this subject is forbidden to Limiteds. So I decided to measure your intelligence, and, to my surprise, I found it measured only six points shy of 1111."

My mouth fell open in astonishment. Now I remembered the day they had put me in the cocoon for the first time, and how Raji had said that the result was six. Back then, I hadn't understood what they were talking about.

"You were born with an IQ of 777," the professor went on. "That's a difference of 334 points. So how did you reduce the difference to only six? The only possible answer is that the knowledge in the books you read increased your intelligence by several hundred points."

"But I was always told that intelligence was like fate or destiny, that we're born with a certain intelligence and we die with it?"

This time, Raji answered. "That's what the government is promoting, in order to allow a small, privileged group to exploit the vulnerable majority, killing every hope they have for change." Then he added, "Yasmina, send IQ report

CHAPTER 18

number 173/56 on the screen to the National Center for Golden Irises. Have them schedule Diyala for the first possible appointment tomorrow for the transplantation of golden irises."

Yasmina was silent for a while, then said, "The first available appointment is tomorrow at 12:20 p.m."

Raji and the professor's faces were both filled with joy. But, as for me, tears filled my eyes, and a strange feeling came over me. It was joy, yes, but lots of other things, too.

"The process is very easy," the professor told me. "It takes only about two minutes, and you won't feel a thing. The main question is: After you get your golden eyes, do you want to go to the finals?"

I sighed. "I can't. I have to help Dima escape the island tomorrow, before the lottery takes place."

"Let's go to the finals," the professor said. "As for Dima, leave that to me."

19

I asked the professor for permission to spend the night in the Burrow, and he said, "Well, I would allow it, if not for your hobby of getting into unfortunate scrapes."

I promised him, in all sincerity, that I would have an uneventful night. Goldens weren't allowed to visit the Burrow, which meant that tomorrow, after my new iris implants, the Burrow would be forbidden to me. So the professor relented and allowed me one last visit.

Dima, Baba, and I got to the square, and we stood waiting our turn for the elevators. Bats hovered overhead as usual, their shadows crisscrossing the square. Every time one of them flew over me, I felt a chill, afraid that it would snatch me and take me away. The wounds I'd gotten on that night from the bamboo stick might heal, sure. But the wounds inside me never would.

The crowd around us was suffocating. As usual, fights broke out because of the exhaustion many people felt after a long day of work. Baba and Dima stood behind me, so that no one would accidentally knock against my sore back. Then it was finally our turn, and we got on the elevator and took the nano-rods down.

CHAPTER 19

I pressed my nose up against the see-through elevator wall, watching as we sank into the heart of the Burrow's endless darkness. The moment I stepped out of the elevator, I was struck by how heavy the air was down on floor -8. What was the air like down on the -60th floor? No wonder the people who lived down there had gray faces and finger-width dark bags under their eyes.

I passed the checkpoint and stood inside the purple circle, where the laser ray passed over my forehead. The professor told me that he had terminated my indenture contract with the bald notary, claiming that I'd repaid my debt. He added that I still had to stay with him and clean his house. Of course I agreed immediately, since I had nowhere else in Quartzia to go! Anyhow, staying with him didn't bother me anymore. I even forgave him for the long hours he made me sit reading books as a punishment. After all, they had the benefit of rapidly boosting my intelligence.

If the professor hadn't put me back into the Limited category, then it would have shown up here that I was an indentured who was outside my approved circle, and they would have arrested me immediately. When the red curtain of light rose in front of me, I hurried to follow Dima and Baba to the stone bridge. I stood at the edge and looked over, into the deep darkness below. Now I knew the scary thing that had happened to me here. It was no longer a mystery—a bat had thrown my mother down into the darkness. Expensive hypnosis had failed to pluck the memory of that day from my mind, but the terror that seized me when I was kidnapped by the bat had been enough to do the job. It was free, too.

A familiar shudder ran through me. Only in a place like the Burrow could one insult from the mouth of a seven-year-old girl be enough to end her mother's life. Dima took my hand and squeezed. She was so happy that I was going to spend the night with her that she'd forgotten her worries over tomorrow's lottery.

We arrived at apartment -879. Baba lay down on his platform after changing his clothes, totally exhausted.

"We're going to spend the night at the café," Dima said. "I want to show you something."

It was hot and my clothes stank of sweat, so Dima gave me some of hers after she'd poured a little of the water that seeped from the rocky wall onto my head and body. Someone knocked on the door, and Dima opened it. It was Hazar, the beauty salon rep. As usual, she was carrying a heavy bag, full of everything we'd seen on the advertisements in the square today.

"We have a special offer from the eye-lens company this month," Hazar said. "Red eyes with a golden sparkle, which you can get for free if you buy any other color. You'll look more Golden than the girls up in Quartzia. Come on, don't miss out!"

"Listen, Hazar," Dima said. "You can take my name off your customer list."

CHAPTER 19

I smiled. Dima had grown up while I'd been away. After that, we hurried to the café. When we got near it, Dima told me to close my eyes. Then she led me forward a few steps and let me open them.

Inside the café, dozens of Einstein holographs floated in the air, repeating, "Don't let anyone else put limits on you. You're the only one who decides how high you can go." I even heard people in the café chanting along.

Dima smiled at me. "When you get to the competition tomorrow, I want you to remember this. Everyone here supports you."

At a table in the middle of the café, I saw our friend Nawal. She waved at me, and we went over to join her. "When Dima told me what happened to you, I was so sorry. He made you into a slave just because you broke his grandmother's bowl? He and his grandma's bowl can both go to hell. So how come you're allowed back down here tonight?"

Her question surprised me, and I wasn't sure what to say.

"Baba paid for the bowl," Dima said. "And of course I chipped in, too."

I asked Nawal why her sister Sabreen wasn't out tonight, and she told me that their parents wouldn't let her go to the café because she'd failed the hair-color shade exam at school. Then Nawal corrected herself: "I mean, to be honest, it wasn't Sabreen's fault. The sat-net service was so patchy and slow that the poor thing spent hours and hours trying to collect the scheduled lessons, but no luck."

Soon, Naru and Nora came in and joined us. Nora apologized for being late. "We got our share of the water today, and it was my turn to do the laundry that had piled up." Naru put in, "As for me, I was watching Episode 635 of *My Love and My Passion*."

My Love and My Passion was the popular Malaysian series that filled screens all across the Burrow. When the waiter came to our table with a tray of energy bars, the other girls took a long time deciding whether to choose mango, frikiwi, or banana—as if there was any difference! Then Naru took out some Marlboro patches from her pocket, and they stuck them to their foreheads. Dima winked at me as she said no thanks. I could tell that she didn't want the girls to let on that she sometimes used the patches, too.

Up in Quartzia, I hadn't seen a single person using patches. Using them was prohibited up top in Quartzia, to protect the health of the Goldens. This visit to the Burrow reminded me of all kinds of things I'd forgotten: problems with the water supply, the slow sat-net, fashion, soap operas, and loads of other things we wasted our lives on. Meanwhile, the Goldens spent their time studying how to create a nutrient gel to preserve their organs, how to grow healthy food, and how to pluck hearts from the chests of the Burrow's young waiters.

CHAPTER 19

Our conversation was interrupted by the familiar competition jingle, and by the display ball that showed an image of Einstein, the Dinosaur of the Sea, and the three other contestants: the Chameleon, Cleopatra, and the Lady of the Cherry Tree. Everyone was silent as their eyes searched for the number of votes that appeared beneath each contestant. Einstein had gotten 78,648 votes, followed by the Dinosaur of the Sea, who'd gotten 25,875. I'd gotten three times as many votes as him!

Someone in the café said, "How did Einstein get less than 80,000 when there are hundreds of thousands of us down here in the Burrow, and every single one of us voted for him?"

Uncle Abu Murad, who owned the café, was the one who answered. "Well, Fahim. That's because every five votes from a Limited is equal to one vote from a Golden."

I remembered General al-Azimi telling the professor, *I want to hear her say, I'm nothing!* In their eyes, we were nothing. The blood in my veins went hot, which made the pain in my back wake up. Then the power suddenly went out. I looked out at the Burrow and saw that everything was dark. The electricity had gone out in the whole Burrow!

"It's not just our floor," I told Dima. "The whole Burrow's gone dark."

Someone near us said, "They cut off the power in the Burrow so we can't vote for Einstein anymore." I believed it.

I apologized to the girls and said I had to go back to our apartment, to spend the rest of the night with Baba. He'd be lonely, because I'd never be able to come here again, and the darkness would make him even sadder. I didn't want him to be sad. I would do whatever it took to bring him and Dima all the knowledge they needed to raise their intelligence, so that one day, they'd live up in Quartzia with me.

I felt my way out of the café and down the corridor. The apartment doors were on my right and the parapet was on my left, overlooking the Burrow's abyss. I looked up, hoping I'd be able to see through the glass dome, up to what the people in Quartzia were doing in the world above. But there was only darkness, so much darkness that I wanted to scream. I wanted to let out a scream that would echo through the whole Burrow, a scream that would say we are NOT nothing, and that we can do ANYTHING, and that pursuing our dreams shouldn't be blocked by a glass dome! But the murmur of bat wings in the air brought me back to my senses.

Just then, an idea flashed through my mind that caused me a few moments of panic before it settled in. But once it did, I felt so sure of it I no longer saw any other way. The professor had stolen my neck, and the general my back . . . and the bat had stolen my mother. I had spent my whole life being robbed of my most precious possessions. And I had surrendered! Now, it was time for someone to stand

CHAPTER 19

up and shout at them: We are not less than you! I would be that person.

Tomorrow, I would go to the competition with pride . . . and with my own chestnut eyes!

20

The government's ceremonial representative hesitated for a long time before he finally gave in and let me ride in the official pumpkin jet with the professor. The professor told the man that he needed me to assist him, and he insisted so firmly that the man finally gave in. The crutch that the professor was leaning on, to feign weakness, sped up the man's agreement. The original plan had been for me to go to the finals with golden eyes. But once I'd decided to keep my own eyes, it became a lot more difficult to get me up to the podium, so the professor had to play the role of a contestant until it came time for the answers.

The moon was no longer full, as it had been on the night of the cruise, but the June weather was beautiful. We passed over the top of Mt Karthala, and I inhaled the sweet scent of the beautiful ylang-ylang flowers that blanketed the slopes of the volcano and everything around it. From the crater of the volcano, a laser projected the words: WELCOME, VISITORS, TO THE QUARTZIA COMPETITION FOR ACADEMIC ADVANCEMENT. The pumpkin jet set us down near the competitors' stage, right in the middle of everything, bypassing the long lines of visitors, who all had to pass through an inspection room, so that the hyena hybrids could sniff them and make sure none of them were carrying a weapon.

CHAPTER 20

Poor Raji, I knew, would have to stand down there in the crowd for a long time. Meanwhile, Dima and Baba would be following things from down in the Burrow, just like the rest of the Limiteds. Retractable display screens were showing the scenes down in the Burrow cafes. My eyes ran over the screens, searching for them, but of course I didn't spot them in the crowds.

There were display balls scattered in all the corners of the field, and giant holograms of our pumpkin jets appeared. The drum of my heart pounded and pounded. The moment we stepped out of our jets, our images appeared on the display balls. The camera followed the professor, although there were a few shots of me, too, with my wavy chestnut hair just a little longer than my shoulders. I was wearing a long-sleeved white sweater with a long sky-blue vest over it, and wide blue-and-white-striped pants. The professor had chosen the pattern from his electronic library; these were clothes from a country called Pakistan, which had existed a hundred years ago, before merging with neighboring countries. The fabric was Egyptian cotton, a gift from one of his students, and the professor had fed it into the electronic tailor along with my measurements and the pattern. Ten minutes later, the clothes had been ready.

The stage had no stairs for us to climb; instead, an employee with black-and-white hair led us to a door beneath the stage. There, a whole team burst out and rushed toward us with combs, brushes, and colors. They pulled the professor away from me after he'd handed me his cane, and they made him sit on a swivel chair. Then they crowded around him, so that only his legs were visible. I stood in a corner, trying to be inconspicuous, but a girl about my age put her hand on my arm, smiled, and whispered, "Should I brighten you up a little? You'll be on camera, too!"

The bad luck collar circled her neck, and the word "Narjis" hung from it. It seemed that this makeup artist, too, was someone unable to pay her debt. Today, the collar of my sweater covered my neck. Underneath, I'd intentionally worn a collar-like necklace that bulged beneath the fabric. I wanted everyone to think I was indentured, since it was clear from the color of my eyes, and from everything else about me, that I wasn't a Golden. A collar would justify my presence in the professor's service.

The Goldens came to enjoy the show with their indentured servants in tow, while the Limiteds returned to the burrow after having completed the service work the Goldens imposed on them. I agreed to the lovely Narjis's offer, so she took me to the side and, without sitting me down, pulled all the tools she needed from a belt around her waist.

"No color on my face, please," I told her. "Just hide the exhaustion a little, if you can."

The girl was surprised by my request. The hair and clothes of the Goldens around us were painted in a thousand shades, and each one of them shone like a meteor in the desert night. Today, I would definitely be the only one with light-colored clothes, plus natural skin and hair.

CHAPTER 20

Quickly, she got to work. Her job wasn't easy, since the past few days had left clear marks on my face, especially around the eyes. When she grasped my shoulder to steady me, I yelped in pain, and she immediately realized why and apologized. We, the indentured, can understand each other without words.

When the professor was ready a few minutes later, Narjis was done with her work, too. I hurried over with the crutch and handed it to him. He looked different from the professor I was used to seeing. Now, his hair radiated out from around his head like the sun, and a spectrum of different shades of gold coated his face. An officer with golden ylang-ylang flowers shining on his shoulders asked the professor for permission to scan him, to check that he wasn't carrying any recording devices, and the professor agreed. When he finished, he nodded at me and asked, "And will she be with you on stage?"

"Yes," the professor said. After that, he asked the professor for permission to check me, too, which he did.

Then, suddenly, General al-Azimi was there in front of us. She gave me a contemptuous look before she said to the professor, "Adam, I am here today in an official capacity, to make sure that everything goes well. As I told you before, be careful what you say. It wasn't easy for me to convince the people who matter that those comments just came out spontaneously. Honestly, I can't protect you any longer."

The professor smiled. "I promise, I won't say a word."

She started to leave, then turned suddenly and asked, "How are you? I was worried about you."

He nodded in response. "I've never been better in my life."

She patted him on the shoulder, right in the place where he'd been struck, and then walked away. What an awful human being. But when the professor turned and looked at me, I saw something in his gaze I'd never seen before—a mix of love, nostalgia, and even pride! I held his arm the way we'd practiced as we climbed the inner steps to the stage. As we emerged out on the surface, images of us swept through the display crystals, showing us as we made our way to the last remaining chair on this side of the podium.

Five chairs had been set up for the contestants. In the first chair was a person who had the head of a very beautiful woman and the body of a giant, hairy, muscular man. In the second chair was an arrogant young man who was sticking his nose up in the air so high, it looked like he might tip over backward. That must be the Dinosaur of the Sea. After that was a plump woman with a kind smile, and finally a woman who looked so old that the professor might be the same age as her children. There was an indentured kneeling on the ground next to her chair, which eased my mind a little. Quartzia's elderly didn't go anywhere without their indentured servants, which meant I wouldn't be the only outsider on the stage.

Opposite the chairs of the five contestants were the chairs of the five judges. Even though they were concealed

CHAPTER 20

in the shadows, I noticed them. I helped the professor into his chair and then knelt beside him. As I looked out at the audience, my eyes fell on General al-Azimi, who was sitting right in the front row. The lights swept back and forth several times, and the professor whispered to me, "I wanted to tell you something. Cancelling your appointment with the National Center for Golden Irises at the last minute was brave, and I respect it."

I didn't think I'd ever had a single word of encouragement from the professor in my entire life, so these words meant a lot to me. These few words chased away the fear that had begun to grow heavy inside me. "Thanks for everything," I whispered back.

Then the sound engineer came around and stuck an ant microphone on the front teeth of each of the contestants. After that the announcer, Sikmadar, came in with a circus of colors, music, applause, and a smile that sparkled with diamonds. He welcomed the audience before he turned to the contestants and said, "In order to preserve the integrity of the competition, none of the viewers or judges will know which of you is the Dinosaur of the Sea, which is Einstein, which is Cleopatra, which is the Chameleon, and which the Lady of the Cherry Tree."

Images of the five avatars filled the display balls, and under each contestant was the number of votes they had gotten. Einstein was still way ahead, despite a two-day power outage down in the Burrow. Now, the number counter under Einstein's image was going up ten at a time, while the others crept up digit by digit. I could never have imagined that the phrase "Don't let anyone else put limits on you" would mean so much to the people in the Burrow.

Then suddenly all the lights in the stadium went out, and a golden spotlight fell only on us. Sikmadar's voice spoke over a background of enthusiastic sounds that was more like rhythmic vibrations than music. He said: "The final question—the one that will determine this year's winner of the title Champion of the Quartzia Competition for Academic Progress—the winner of five million binars, and the winner of the Medal of Intelligence is . . . "

He was silent for several long seconds. I straightened up, even though my knees stayed on the ground. Every cell in my body opened up. I could almost hear the engines in my brain revving up and the adrenaline flowing through my veins. I could've traced it with my finger.

And the announcer said: "What digit appears most frequently, in the numbers from one to a thousand?"

I didn't need to count up all the numbers to get the answer; instead, I had to extract the pattern. I knew the answer and poked the professor, so he reached out and hit the button. But his movement was too slow—the Dinosaur of the Sea had gotten to his button first. His *ring* cut through the air a fraction of a second before mine.

"I'm sorry," the professor whispered. "So sorry."

My chest filled and emptied a thousand times, my vocal cords spasmed, and I could no longer speak. The lights brightened, and Sikmadar's voice said, "We won't say the

CHAPTER 20

name of the avatar until we're absolutely certain of the answer. Go ahead, fourth contestant, give us the answer."

The Dinosaur of the Sea's cheeks puffed up as he said, "Zero."

He was wrong! I whispered to the professor, "He's wrong."

The smile disappeared from Sikmadar's face, and he said, "I'm sorry, my friend, but that is incorrect. We now pass the question to the other contestants." The professor slammed his button as fast as he could.

"We will not give the name of the avatar until we are certain of a correct answer," Sikmadar said. "Contestant number five, go ahead."

The professor looked at me. I was still on my knees, so now I stood up, and he took the ant microphone off his tooth and handed it to me. I stuck it to my tooth and said, "The number one appears most frequently."

"That is a correct answer," Sikmadar said. "But . . ." The stadium went quiet, as though an icy wind had just passed through, freezing everyone inside. "The indentured have no right to participate in the competition."

"I am not indentured," I said. "I'm a free—"

He cut in: "No one can answer except 2114442."

"I am 2114442," I said. "I was the one who operated Einstein."

A gasp came from the stands around us, and the air seemed to crackle all the way up to the sky. My image filled all the display balls.

Sikmadar wiped the sweat from his forehead and said, "I mean . . . The competition is limited to . . . to the . . . "

Now, the Dinosaur of the Sea broke in "The Limiteds have no right to be outside the Burrow after five in the afternoon. What are you doing here among your betters? Arrest her!"

General al-Azimi stood and said, in a voice that dripped with arrogance, "Yes, if you are not indentured, then you have no right to be here. I'll call the guards."

She swiped at the disc on her wrist, and bats appeared in the sky. The professor shouted, "She is Golden, and her IQ report is on file under the ID 173/56."

Instantly, the monitors showed my photo and my IQ report on file at the National Center for Golden Irises. How had they gotten it so quickly?

"But this girl has chestnut eyes," Sikmadar said.

"This girl's name is Diyala Karthala," I said. "And chestnut is my favorite color."

The audience erupted with a mix of joyful laughter and jeers.

"Why didn't you sit in one of the contestant's chairs?" Sikmadar asked. "It seems you meant to deceive us."

CHAPTER 20

"The professor can't sit on the floor because of an accident he had two days ago," I said.

The half-man, half-woman contestant asked, "Why did you bring him with you on stage?"

"So that he can help me," I said. "I also had an accident two days ago."

"I serve her, and she serves me," the professor said.

Angry cries rang out through the stands. They couldn't stand the idea of a Golden serving someone with chestnut-colored eyes. Confusion spread through the audience. "Liar!" I heard, and "Cheater!" and "Kick her out of here!" Most of them seemed so full of loathing that it scared me. What had I ever done to these people to make them hate me? The professor squeezed my hand, and I felt a little better. Then I heard Raji's voice, coming to me from the audience: "You're the smartest one here, Chestnut!" I smiled.

Sikmadar spent a long time whispering with the judges before he came over to me and said, "All right, Diyala. To be honest, you don't fit the criteria we're used to on this program. You're young, and you . . . Well, in order to be sure you're not hiding something, we'll have to ask you one final question. If you can answer it, the prize will be yours."

The kind-looking fat woman called out, "That's not fair! The girl just answered, and the prize is hers."

"I'll do it," I told Sikmadar.

He smiled. "All right, then I need to ask you to come here. The scanner will make sure you're not carrying any transmission devices."

I went to where he'd pointed. Then, when he waved his hand, two Golden men walked up to me with their scanning devices. They circled me several times, until green lights popped up on their devices. Then they left.

I stood next to Sikmadar as the question appeared on the screen in front of me:

The tickets sold for today's competition each have four numbers on them. Among them are lucky cards, in which the sum of the first two numbers is equal to the sum of the second two. How many lucky cards does our audience have today?

I swallowed, and the sound echoed through all the speakers. Silence fell. I tapped my foot. The question made no sense to me. I closed my eyes, and the Dinosaur of the Sea's shout rang in my ears, "She's a fake!"

Then I heard the general's voice, distant and echoey, as though coming from the bottom of a well: "She's a nothing."

I opened my eyes and looked at her. Then the solution spread out in front of my eyes, like the wild jellyfish I'd seen through the glass bottom of the boat. I smiled and said, "Today, there are 385 lucky cards."

The judges cheered, "Well done!" Then Sikmadar turned and pointed at me as he said, "Braaaaavooo!" There was applause from the audience. At first, it was faint and timid,

CHAPTER 20

but the sound soon increased until it became louder than the roar of the sea.

I looked straight at the general and said, "Chestnut eyes can do anything."

At that, she stood up, mounted the stage, and grabbed the ant microphone from Sikmadar's pocket and affixed it to her tooth. She said: "No one would like to see Diyala win today's title more than me. However, I'm sorry to report that I have just been informed by the wise leadership of our island that one of the requirements for participants in the Quartzia competitions is that they must have both a Golden father and a Golden mother. And sadly, for Diyala that is not the case. Her father, a Limited, works as a cook in the professor's house. So perhaps we should continue posing questions to the remaining contestants until one of them wins."

The fat lady stood up. "I withdraw."

Tears filled my eyes. I couldn't feel the tears, but I could see them in the dozens of display balls that were scattered all around us. Sikmadar looked at me in confusion, then said, "I apologize, but the law is the law, and . . ."

Then the professor stood. He pried open my lips with his index finger and thumb, pulled the ant microphone off my front tooth, and stuck it in his mouth. "Diyala has a Golden father and a Golden mother." I clapped my hands over my eyes. My father was a cook and my mother had been a painter. Their eyes were a million miles away from golden. And I was proud of them for who they were!

Why was the professor saying this? Gently, he pulled a hand off one of my eyes and raised it up. "I present to you Diyala al-Azizi, my daughter. I am Professor Adam al-Azizi, and her mother was Alaa Alati. We are Diyala's Golden mother and father."

General al-Azimi barked out a laugh. "Alaa's daughter? Nice try, professor."

The professor looked into her eyes. "Would you like me to prove it?"

"Please do," she said, with a challenge in her eyes.

Silence fell so hard, it was as if the tens of thousands of attendees had suddenly disappeared. The professor said, "My wife, Alaa Alati, gave birth to Diyala, who registered an intelligence of 777. Of course, that meant our daughter was doomed to live in the Burrow, but her mother refused to send her there alone. So we parted ways—I stayed up above while she went to live with our daughter in the Burrow. Later, my daughter was adopted by a noble man named al-Karthala, and she took his name. And, contrary to the common belief that intelligence is fixed, she has proven that continuous reading will increase it!"

A long, "Noooooo!" sounded from the audience, and they threw out a barrage of angry comments, including, "Impossible!" and "Liar!" and "Traitor!" But the professor didn't care. He went on: "While she worked in my home, Diyala also spent years reading in my library. Today, her IQ is 1119. And so the story ends. DNA tests can confirm everything I've said."

CHAPTER 20

General al-Azimi butted in: "I find this story difficult to believe." At just that moment, some of the screens were showing what was happening down in the Burrow cafes. The general appeared upset for a moment before the transmission was cut off. But the residents of the Burrow wouldn't remain silent in the face of all this injustice, and the counters under my image were turning so rapidly, they looked like a fan. Today, my mission had succeeded. Whatever happened, the residents of the Burrow had hope.

General al-Azimi walked up to us, pulled the microphone out of her mouth, and whispered to me and the professor, "*You* are still a nothing, and *you,* professor, are going to pay. Tomorrow, we will announce that the DNA tests show that your story was a fraud."

The professor also removed his microphone. "General al-Azimi, my analysis has shown that your baby nephew will also be a Limited. So, if you don't want me to tell the audience about it, I hope you'll agree that our story is true."

She lifted a palm, gesturing to her bats as she hissed, "I will bury you a thousand feet underground before you can even say a word."

He crossed his arms. "I've already fed the information to Houdini's satellite. If anything happens to me, the moon will broadcast that the son of the president of Quartzia will not be a Golden, and every citizen in Quartzia will know it."

Houdini's satellite broadcasts from a parallel galaxy, so Earth-based jammers had no effect on it. The general's eyelids pinched shut, like an owl with a cold. She dismissed the bats that were hovering above us and muttered, "My bat should have turned you and your daughter into carbon ash."

She glared at us for a few seconds before she put the ant back on her tooth and plastered on a smile. She took my hand and said, "Although the story is strange, Professor Adam's integrity is beyond doubt. Diyala al-Azizi has given hope to the citizens of Quartzia, and we will be glad if our brothers and sisters down in the Burrow can raise their intelligence as Diyala has, so that we can all contribute, hand in hand, to the glorious future of our beloved nation."

The Dinosaur of the Sea stood up and kicked over his chair before he stomped off the stage. The kind woman came over and kissed me, and the judges surrounded me with their congratulations. Even Narjis came up and gave me an affectionate hug. The display balls and screens came back to life, showing that the people down in the Burrow were singing, dancing, and throwing their hats in the air with joy.

Sikmadar spread his arms, and on the display bottle in front of him, there appeared: "Diyala al-Azizi, bank balance: 5,000,000 binars."

Then he announced: "Diyala has just become one of the wealthiest people in the city. In her bank account, which we have just now opened on her behalf, the Competitions Department has placed five million binars for her to use as she likes."

CHAPTER 20

Every cell in my body bloomed with pleasure, so that the oxygen in my lungs was no longer enough for all of them. But then I remembered the lottery, which spoiled my happiness.

"What about the Dreamland Lottery?" I whispered to the professor.

"Listen to what Sikmadar has to say."

The music stopped, the lights went out, and then the spotlight returned to Sikmadar. "As for the Dreamland lottery, we must apologize," he said. "It's been cancelled this season due to overcrowding."

I lifted the professor's hand to my lips and kissed it. After all, wasn't he my father? "How did you do it?" I asked.

"Yesterday, I told General al-Azimi that I'd developed a liquid that preserves the organs of those who have been dead for ten years in the organ bank. That means there will be enough organs available for everyone."

"Did you really develop a fluid like that?"

"What do you think we were working on in the lab all those years?"

I hugged him. "Thanks, Father." He hugged me back tightly, but it didn't hurt. This was the first thing I had learned about my biological father: his hugs didn't cause back pain.

21

That night, I sat with my new-found father in the light of the "Tree of Eternal Virtue," which he had created so that it was half-covered in leaves shaped like silver hearts, and half-covered with purple needles.

"I never really thanked you for saving my life," I said.

"I failed you on the day you were born, and nothing I do will ever make up for that. Your mother Alaa was a much better person than I. A truly great person. She was twenty years younger than me, and, when I met her, I had completely given up on meeting someone. I fell in love with her, and it was a love like no other. And since the day your mother left this house, I haven't been happy for a single moment."

"What happened? Tell me . . ."

He put his feet into the fishpond, and the new squirrel-tailed fish darted away. He let out a long sigh, and then said, "When I read your intelligence report on the day you were born, I couldn't believe my eyes. I had engineered you very precisely, but I didn't find any of what I'd planned. It felt as if God were sending me a message that His will remains above all scientific endeavors."

CHAPTER 21

The professor's knee began to jiggle nervously, and I could see he was in pain. But he went on, "I spent most of my life earning the Quartzia Gene Editing Lab its excellent reputation. Your existence would have made me lose my standing as a geneticist, so we wrote on your birth certificate that your father was unknown. Quartzian law is clear: only Goldens can sleep up above, on its land. It was inevitable that you would be sent to the Burrow. But your mother refused to be separated from you."

The image of Mama clinging to me on the day the bat had seized me flashed into my mind, bringing tears to my eyes.

"Your mother decided to leave me so she could live down in the Burrow with you," he said. "She had her golden irises replaced with blue ones, and down there, she met the noble Karthala. Much like Mt. Karthala, Nabil is generous and kind, and so she married him—without him ever knowing she was a Golden. Then he officially adopted you, and you took his name. Diyala Karthala.

"Alaa would come to me every month for money, so that you could have a comfortable life. In exchange, she would bring me her paintings, and I pretended to sell them, although in reality I kept them all hanging in the shed."

I remembered the days Mama used to come home, at the beginning of each month, with everything we wanted. I remembered warm food, colors, the smell of Baba's dishes, and lots of laughs.

"Alaa told me about the cruel injustices of the bats down in the Burrow, and I knew how proud she was. That's why I made the repair ointment—I was afraid that, one day, she would stand up to a bat and feel the sting of its whip. The ointment was made from cells from your umbilical cord, which we saved from the day you were born. That's why it worked so well on my wound—because it carries my genetic material, too."

The box had the letters AA on it: Alaa Alati. The comb, too. I smiled. "That means I was the one who saved *your* life on the day I ran away, not the other way around."

I took a piece of cake made with dates, walnuts, and pomegranate juice that I'd brought out from the kitchen for our little celebration, and I offered him a piece. He waved it away, seemingly overwhelmed by memories.

"Then the day I feared came, and your mother didn't show up at the end of the month," he said. "I asked after her and found out she'd disappeared. I searched for her in hospitals and in prisons, but there was no trace of her."

He swallowed hard and went on: "A thousand times, she made me swear to take care of you if anything happened to her, although I would not have abandoned my daughter, even if I had not made a promise to Alaa. When I despaired of Alaa ever returning, I sent word to your neighbor that I needed employees, and that's how you ended up here."

I remembered the day our neighbor Kawthar had come to tell Baba about the generous offer, encouraging him to

CHAPTER 21

take it. Back then, a crocodile hadn't yet eaten her arm, and she had clapped her hands when Baba agreed.

"Is that why you were so hard on me? Because I was the reason Mama left you?"

He winced as he gave a slow nod. "At first, yes, that's how it was. But then I started to love you, little by little, against my will."

I let out a yelp of laughter. "What kind of love was that exactly? Criticism, blame, and punishments every day."

"Nabil was very permissive with you, so I felt a sense of responsibility for your upbringing. I had to shake the dust of the Burrow off you, since the people down there talk too much, achieve too little, are sloppy and ignorant—"

"The people down in the Burrow aren't motivated because they don't have any hope," I cut in. "Do you know what motivated me to read? It was something you said to me on my first day of work. You told me that my salary would be 125 binar, which I would receive every 25 days. I asked you, 'So how much will I make each day?' That day, you gave me a look of grave disappointment, and you said, 'You're seven years old and don't know how to divide?'"

"I remember it so clearly," he said. "That very same day, I asked you to clean the shelves in the library, hoping some book would catch your attention."

Now, I flopped down in the grass and sighed. "I found a series of twenty math books called *Numbers from Adam to Einstein,* and I started reading them. Einstein's been my friend for a long time."

"And things went on like that for years, until one day, I needed information from an old statistics book, but I couldn't find it on the shelf. I thought that perhaps you hadn't been returning the books to their proper places after cleaning, and I intended to dock your salary. But then the book returned to its proper place the next day, and it didn't seem like a coincidence. I took a photo of the books before you arrived and after you left, and—after comparing the photos—I realized that you were borrowing my books. How did you dare?"

"Believe me, I was sick with fear every single morning. And after my run-in with the bats, I know how stupid it was."

Now, he asked Yasmina to turn off all the garden lights except for the soft violet bio-bulbs. Yasmina also turned off the fountains, so that we were surrounded only by the sounds of crickets, the scent of sea breeze in our hair, and the sight of Mt. Karthala gazing down at us.

"On the day I caught you, I told you that smuggling books was dangerous, and you told me that nothing in the world could stop you from reading. *Then* you threatened to make a fake gold card so that you could borrow books from the Quartzia Public Library. Good grief, my girl. If the elevator bats didn't catch you, the library bats certainly would."

CHAPTER 21

I remembered the moment I'd told him my idea of going to the library, and how he'd slapped his hands together and said, *Young lady, have you lost your mind?*

"I wasn't sure what to do," he said. "I had to protect you. Then I had an idea—the only way to stop your smuggling activities was to keep you in my house. And, for you to sleep in Quartzia, I had to indenture you. I thought that having a comfortable life and a library to satisfy your curiosity would be enough to keep you here forever. I ordered you to call me Sir, hoping that you'd get used to your new situation, and I added the cleaning responsibilities to distract you from your worries. After that, I discovered your burgeoning mathematical genius. And when I saw how much your intelligence had changed since your birth, a beautiful hope bloomed inside me.

"I started sending you to the library every day so that your intelligence would rise faster and you could get golden eyes legally. When that happened, I planned to give you your freedom back. Then you could read as much as you pleased and live here . . . with me!"

I picked up the thread of the story: "I started planning my escape from the very first day of my indenture. I was going to find some money in the house and run away. But after I saw the bats up close, on the day they visited you, I was too afraid to run away. So I decided that, instead, I'd win the Quartzia competition in order to repay my debt and leave the country."

"And then you had Einstein make that comment that almost ruined our entire household," he said. "I had to quickly lift your intelligence so that you'd become a Golden, with full rights and privileges. Who knew what they'd do if they found out the contestant inciting people with such statements was an indentured servant!"

"Was that why you threw me down in the basement with those books?"

"I didn't have a choice. I needed you to be trapped somewhere, so you had nothing to do but read for a long period. It had occurred to me that perhaps sparking different areas in your brain—such as those that process thought on literature, drawing, music, and geography—might lead to your intelligence increasing even faster. And indeed, that was the case."

Dawn was beginning to break, and the cold air made our recovering bodies ache. We both got up and headed toward the house.

"I feel like my whole life was leading me to one moment, the one I was up there on that stage," I said. "The moment when I confronted the people who'd put limits on me and chose my own limits. If I'd gone there with golden eyes and won, then my victory would've been another feather in the cap of the Goldens and an insult to everyone down in the Burrow."

The breeze coming off the sea was cold, so he put his arm around me. "Alaa loved the people in the Burrow, and

CHAPTER 21

she would never have stood in your way. I agreed out of respect for her."

"I love the Burrow, too. I decided to use my prize money to broadcast all the scientific knowledge we have to Houdini's satellite, since then it can reach all the homes in the Burrow. That way, for the people there, it will be as if they have access to the great Professor Adam's library."

Suddenly, the violet bio-lights that had been illuminating the garden went out. My father turned to me, "It looks like you forgot to apply the gel that nourishes the glow bacteria, yes? Did you think you'd get away with such negligence?"

I laughed. "Changing the gel was my job on one of the days you locked me up down in the basement. Did you think you could get away with that without paying a price?"

Our laughter filled the house. The first rays of the sun had begun to peek out from beyond the horizon. The gate opened, and Baba and Dima walked through. Dima called out, "For the first time ever, we rode the elevator alone—we were there for its first trip of the morning. We came early to congratulate you, so congratulations, congratulations, congratulations!" Then she hugged me.

Baba, of course, didn't say a word, but instead he opened his arms, and I melted into the warmth of his embrace. Would the bald notary allow me to register my name as Diyala Karthala al-Azizi?

Raji also came in through the garden's side gate. He joined us, carrying bottles of a celebratory coconut drink.

"Here you go, everyone! Coconut juice!"

"Yasmina," I said, "have the dancing ice fish bring us out some ice."

"Yes, ma'am," she answered.

I smiled. "Thanks," I told her, before adding, "my friend."

www.ingramcontent.com/pod-product-compliance
Lightning Source LLC
Chambersburg PA
CBHW031436090525
26348CB00012B/18